She'd already fallen for ~~Hart Fisher~~ ago...

Even before he'd save~~d~~

She was helpless to fig~~ht~~
was helpless to fight th~~at~~ ~~over~~powered her.
She'd nearly lost him—nearly lost her opportunity to
ever be this close to him. When he laid her down on a
bed, she clung to him, pulling him down on top of her
like he'd been that night he'd sneaked into her room.

Their legs tangled, and she felt the evidence of his
passion. She moaned and arched against him.

"Wendy..." he murmured as he tried to ease back—
away from her.

She might have let him go—if she didn't see the
desire on his face, which was flushed, his eyes
glittering. He wanted her, too.

She moved her hand between them, over the fly of
his worn jeans. His breath hissed out between his
clenched teeth.

"You're killing me," he murmured.

She shook her head. "No. I don't want that to happen.
I want you..."

Alive.

* * *

**Be sure to check out the previous books in the
exciting Bachelor Bodyguards miniseries.**

* * *

**If you're on Twitter, tell us what you
think of Harlequin Romantic Suspense!
#harlequinromsuspense**

Dear Reader,

I'm excited to bring you another story about the Bachelor Bodyguards! If you read *Guarding His Witness*, you know that the Payne Protection Agency has a dangerous new assignment. Drug kingpin and killer Luther Mills has sworn out a contract against everyone who can put him behind bars—where he deserves to be—for the rest of his life. Fortunately, the police chief brought in the Payne Protection Agency to make sure nobody is hurt before the trial.

In *Evidence of Attraction*, he ramps up his efforts to get his charges dismissed by trying to have the evidence against him destroyed. But despite the threats crime scene investigator Wendy Thompson has been receiving, she is too committed to her job and justice to compromise either. Bodyguard Hart Fisher has his work cut out for him, though. To prevent Luther's leak in the police department from finding out the chief is on to them, Hart has to pose as Wendy's boyfriend. When Wendy begins to bond with the single dad's young daughter, Hart has to keep reminding himself it's just an assignment— maybe the most dangerous one of his life.

Hope you enjoy this latest installment of Bachelor Bodyguards!

Happy reading!

Lisa Childs

EVIDENCE OF ATTRACTION

Lisa Childs

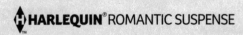

HARLEQUIN® ROMANTIC SUSPENSE

Recycling programs
for this product may
not exist in your area.

ISBN-13: 978-1-335-66228-6

Evidence of Attraction

Copyright © 2019 by Lisa Childs

Printed in U.S.A.

Ever since **Lisa Childs** read her first romance novel (a Harlequin story, of course) at age eleven, all she wanted was to be a romance writer. With over forty novels published with Harlequin, Lisa is living her dream. She is an award-winning, bestselling romance author. Lisa loves to hear from readers, who can contact her on Facebook, through her website, lisachilds.com, or her snail-mail address, PO Box 139, Marne, MI 49435.

Books by Lisa Childs

Harlequin Romantic Suspense

Colton 911

Colton 911: Baby's Bodyguard

Bachelor Bodyguards

His Christmas Assignment
Bodyguard Daddy
Bodyguard's Baby Surprise
Beauty and the Bodyguard
Nanny Bodyguard
Single Mom's Bodyguard
In the Bodyguard's Arms
Soldier Bodyguard
Guarding His Witness
Evidence of Attraction

The Coltons of Red Ridge

Colton's Cinderella Bride

Top Secret Deliveries

The Bounty Hunter's Baby Surprise

The Coltons of Shadow Creek

The Colton Marine

Visit the Author Profile page at Harlequin.com for more titles.

Chapter 1

Lose the evidence or lose your life...

That was the first threat Wendy Thompson had received, tucked behind the windshield wiper on her car. When she'd seen the slip of paper, she'd thought it was a flyer for a new restaurant or a dry cleaner. Of course, as an evidence tech, she'd processed the paper for prints. The couple of very smudged partials she'd recovered had been insufficient for her to match in AFIS, the Automated Fingerprint Identification System.

The next threat she'd received a few weeks later had been a phone call, the voice of the caller a hoarse, unidentifiable whisper. *Lose the evidence or lose everything and everybody you love...*

She shivered as she replayed the call in her head as she had so many times since receiving it two days ago. Even though she hadn't recognized the caller's voice, she knew who was behind the threats. She knew which ballistics and DNA reports, despite all the cases she handled, that someone didn't want making to trial. Because she knew that, she also knew the threats weren't idle.

She hadn't slept since receiving that call, and she worried she wouldn't sleep tonight, either. She had been lying awake in the dark for hours. She'd already kicked off the blankets, but now that she was shivering, she pulled them back up over her panties and the oversize T-shirt she wore as a nightgown. Maybe she should shut the window, but it was a few feet away, so she would have to walk across the creaky floor to reach it. The noise might awaken her parents, who weren't used to someone else being in the house.

They already suspected something was wrong because she'd come home the night she'd received that call. She'd claimed her apartment was being fumigated for cockroaches, and they'd seemed to buy that explanation—until she'd started checking locks on the windows and doors. She hoped she'd convinced them that was just a habit she'd developed since living alone.

She hadn't locked her window, though, because her old bedroom was on the second floor. Her parents had moved their bedroom to the den on the main floor since Mom's knee replacement surgery a month ago. Wendy probably should have slept down there, as well—to protect them—but then they would have known for certain that something was going on. And she didn't want to worry them.

She had reported the threats to the chief of the River City Police Department, though, and he'd ordered a patrol car stationed on the quiet suburban street. The officers would notice if there was anyone suspicious in the area. At this hour, anyone outside would be suspicious.

But Wendy felt better being here herself, her service weapon within easy reach on the bedside table. While not all police departments armed their crime scene technicians, River City PD had. Not too long ago, the southwestern Michigan city, which was even bigger than Detroit, had been as corrupt and lawless as the cities in the old Westerns her father watched. And, of course, crime scenes were usually in the most dangerous areas of the city. The FBI had stepped in years ago to help clean up the city, but it wasn't really safe.

Not yet…

Getting legendary drug kingpin Luther Mills off the street would help. He was in jail, awaiting trial. But he needed to be in prison—a maximum security one—for the rest of his life. That would only happen if the evidence against him made it to trial.

And it would—despite the threats Wendy had received. They had to be from Mills. Or, since he was in jail, from someone working for him. Unfortunately, he had many, many people working for him.

That was why she needed to be here, to make sure her parents stayed safe. Along with some friends, they were the only real loved ones she had—besides her job. Maybe it was because she loved *it* so much that she had no other loved ones. She was only twenty-seven, though, and eventually work would let up, when crime and Luther Mills went down, and she would have more time for dating.

If she found someone she actually wanted to date, she would make time now, though. But she hadn't found anyone yet.

A face flashed into her mind. A handsome face with chiseled features: strong jaw, sharp cheekbones, deep brown eyes that could stare right into a person's soul. Not hers, though...

Hart Fisher had never even looked at her. Of course, he had been married some of his time with the River City PD. But after he had left the vice unit and become a detective, he and his wife had divorced. He would have been available then...if he had ever showed any interest in Wendy. But he hadn't.

Not too long after his divorce, he had resigned from the force. Wendy had heard he was working for a former coworker, Parker Payne, as a bodyguard.

She expelled a wistful sigh. She wouldn't have minded him guarding her body. At least then he might have to look at her. But would he like what he saw?

Untamable red hair and freckles that showed even through the heaviest application of makeup. She uttered another sigh. This one was of resignation. If the rumors around the station were true, his ex had been a beauty queen—a former Miss River City—so it was no wonder Hart had never noticed Wendy.

All a woman like Wendy could do was dream about a man like Hart Fisher, and after his divorce, she had often dreamed about him. About him kissing her, touching her…even just smiling at her.

Her sigh turned to a yawn. The past few sleepless nights must have caught up with her because her eyelids grew heavy. With the officers stationed outside, she didn't need to worry. Her parents would be safe. She could sleep and dream…of a certain former River City PD detective.

But she hadn't been asleep for long when a noise awoke her. The hardwood floor emitted a low creaking sound, as if someone was walking across it. Had her dad come upstairs to close her window? She could still feel the wind, though, blowing through the sheer curtains and across her body. And the sound was coming toward her, not away from her.

She jerked fully awake and reached for her Glock. But before she was able to grab it, a strong hand grabbed her, wrapping tightly around her wrist. She stared up at the dark shadow looming over her bed. Before she could open her mouth to scream, the shadow's other hand covered her lips. She thrashed, kicking out, trying to fight.

But then the shadow dropped heavily onto her, a hard body covering hers. She kept thrashing around, trying to get her knee to connect where it would hurt him most. From the grunts slipping through his lips and his overpowering strength, she knew her intruder was male.

It had to be one of Luther's minions sent to deliver the next threat in person. The first had been paper, the second the call and now…this one…

Was he just supposed to threaten her? Or was he supposed to make good on those threats and kill her?

If that was his intention, she wasn't going to make it easy for him. Wendy Thompson wasn't going out without one hell of a fight.

"Stop," Hart Fisher whispered, pressing his mouth close to Wendy Thompson's ear. Her soft hair tickled his lips. "Stop fighting me."

If she kneed him again, he might not be able to stop himself from crying out.

"You were supposed to be expecting me," he whispered. Somebody—either his boss or hers—had said they would call and let her know he was coming. When she hadn't been waiting outside for him, he hadn't wanted to wake her parents. He had also wanted to see how easily he could get past her supposed protection stationed outside the house.

Too easily.

He shivered and so did Wendy, her body shuddering beneath his. Unfortunately, his body was reacting to the closeness of hers, to her warmth, her softness, her scent...

She smelled sweet, like vanilla.

If she kneed him again, it was going to hurt even more than it already had. Even though she should have been expecting him, she kept thrashing around beneath him.

"Stop," he told her again even though she had stilled, her body tense beneath his. "I'm here to protect you."

Her lips moved under his hand, brushing over his skin as she tried to talk. At least, he hoped that was all she was going to do—not scream.

"I'm Hart Fisher." He identified himself before moving his hand away from her mouth.

"I know *who* you are," she said in a raspy whisper. "What I need to know is *what* the hell you are doing in my bed."

Heat rushed back to his face from where it had pooled in other parts of his body. Had she felt his reaction to her closeness?

He quickly moved off her, hoping that she hadn't. It had been too damn long since he'd been with a woman if just any female could affect him like that.

But Wendy Thompson wasn't just any female. She was the one he'd been assigned to protect. He needed to focus on that, on protecting her.

But now he realized he might also need to protect himself. "I was trying to stop you from shooting me. I work for the Payne Protection Agency," he said.

She nodded. "Parker Payne."

"Yes," he said. Until this assignment, Hart had thought Parker was his friend as well as his boss. Now he wasn't so damn sure. "I was assigned to protect you. The chief or Parker was supposed to call to let you know I was coming over tonight."

She reached toward her nightstand again, but instead of grabbing her Glock, she picked up her cell. The screen lit up with a notification that she had a voice mail— undoubtedly from the chief or Parker.

"I already have protection," Wendy said. "I have the whole River City PD looking out for me."

Hart snorted derisively. He hadn't been surprised that Luther Mills had got to someone in the police department. Despite the FBI's efforts over the past few years to clean it up, there was still too much corruption in the force.

She bristled in defense and said, "They are my fellow officers."

He knew that, as well as getting her master's degree in criminal science, she had also graduated from the police academy. Because of that, she had the respect of the rest of the precinct. But that respect meant nothing now, since she had been the one who'd collected the evidence against Luther Mills.

"I know," he said. "But that doesn't mean you can trust them."

"What?" she asked, her voice rising sharply above a whisper. She lowered it and continued. "What the hell are you insinuating?"

"I'm not insinuating anything," he said. "I'm telling you that Luther Mills got to someone within the police department. That's why the chief hired the Payne Protection Agency to step in and provide security for everyone associated with Mills's upcoming trial."

"No..." She shook her head, tumbling her wild red curls around her face. "I just talked to Chief Lynch a few days ago and he said nothing about hiring a bodyguard for me."

Hart narrowed his eyes at the suspicion in her voice. Did she think he was the one Luther Mills had got to? She must have because she started reaching for her gun again. He caught her wrist. Her pulse leaped beneath his fingers. "If you would have picked up the call you missed, you would have known I am here to take you to a meeting with the chief."

"In the middle of the night?" She snorted now, like he had earlier. "Yeah, right. How much is Mills paying you?"

Hart felt like she'd kneed him again, but this time her sharp knee struck him right in his pride.

"That's ridiculous," he said, not caring that his voice got a little louder with anger. He'd spent years in the vice unit trying to build a case against the notorious drug dealer. But every time anyone had got close to prosecuting Luther Mills, the eyewitnesses and the evidence had disappeared. "I am not working for Mills!"

Wendy shushed him now.

So he lowered his voice when he added, "But someone in the RCPD is, which puts your life and the lives of everyone else involved in his prosecution in danger. That's why the chief wants to meet with everybody at Payne Protection tonight, so that he can explain everything."

She shook her head again. "You're crazy if you think I'm going anywhere with you."

Back when he was on the force, other officers had teased him that the red-haired evidence tech had a crush on him. He'd laughed off their claims then and it was clear now that they'd just been messing with him. Wendy Thompson couldn't have had a crush on him since she didn't even trust him.

Not that he blamed her. Luther Mills wanted her dead, so she shouldn't trust anyone. But there was one person even more above suspicion than Hart. He reached for his phone. "Play that voice mail on your phone. Or better yet, I'll call Parker. The chief is with him. Lynch will verify he called this meeting."

Before he could pull the phone from his pocket, her bedroom door flew open. Light flooded the space, illuminating the pink walls and frilly curtains of a little girl's bedroom. *Felicity would love this room.* Pain clenched his heart at the thought of his daughter.

Would he ever see her again?

He was not so sure at the moment because that light also glinted off the gun in the hand of the man standing in the doorway.

Hart might have been called in too late to save Wendy Thompson.

Or himself…

Parker opened the door to the room off his wife's office at the Payne Protection Agency. A little girl lay asleep in one of the beds in the nursery Sharon had designed for their children. She'd wanted them close while she and Parker worked. But this child wasn't theirs.

Her hair was pale blond. Her skin was pale, as well. She didn't look like Hart Fisher's kid, either. She was tiny and delicate-looking, despite her fierce grasp on the rag doll clasped against her side.

Sharon had opened up the nursery for any of the bodyguards to use for their children. She loved kids so much that the former nanny would willingly care for any and all. And this little girl, already abandoned by her mother, needed extra care.

She needed her father.

Maybe Parker shouldn't have sent Hart off on this assignment. Sure, Hart had chosen to become a bodyguard and it was probably safer, as well as more flexible, than being on the River City Police Department.

Except for this assignment.

From his years working in the RCPD's vice unit, Parker personally knew how dangerous Luther Mills could be. The infamous drug dealer was determined not to go to trial, and he would kill anyone and everyone who got in his way. By protecting the evidence tech, Hart was definitely getting in his way. Again.

It wasn't the first time Hart had made life more difficult for Luther. Like Parker, he'd tried for years to shut down Mills's illegal business and send the ruthless criminal to prison. Right now Luther was only going after those associated with his trial. But what if he went after anyone who'd ever tried to take him down?

Then Parker was in danger, too, and so was every member of his franchise of the Payne Protection Agency. He'd hired all former vice cops for his team.

Parker pulled his cell from his pocket and glanced at the time on the screen.

Hart should have been back, with Wendy Thompson, by now. Her parents' house, where she'd told the chief she was staying, wasn't that far from the agency's office.

Where were they? If they were running late, Hart would have called to let him know. The only reason he would not have called was that he was not able to.

Maybe Luther had already made good on his threat against Wendy. But if he'd taken her out, he would have had to take out her bodyguard along with her.

Chapter 2

Fear shot through Wendy. But she wasn't afraid of the man who'd entered her bedroom with his gun drawn. She was afraid that the two men in her room would kill each other. Hart was already reaching for his weapon as he tried shoving Wendy behind him for her protection.

But who would protect him?

"Daddy!" she yelled as she jumped between the men and their guns. "Don't shoot!" She held a hand out to each of them, pushing Hart back as she held off her father. "Either of you! Don't shoot each other!"

Her father blinked dark eyes that were still bleary with sleep as he focused on her and the stranger in her bedroom. "What's going on, Wendy? Who the hell is he?"

"He's my…my…" She couldn't say "bodyguard" because her father's next question would be why she needed one. And she didn't want to tell her father about Luther Mills and the threats. Not yet. She trusted the police department to keep them safe. But if Hart was telling the truth and someone within the department couldn't be trusted…then she might have to tell her father, to implore him and her mother to leave town until after the trial. As long as she didn't have to worry about them, she would be fine.

Despite Luther Mills and those threats, she didn't need a bodyguard. She didn't *need* Hart Fisher. But since he was there, in her bedroom, in the middle of the night, she needed to explain his presence.

"Wendy?" her father prodded.

She felt like a teenager who'd been caught necking on the living room couch with her boyfriend. Except her father had never caught her with anyone when she was a teenager. She'd been too busy studying back then.

"Boyfriend," she blurted out. "He's my boyfriend." Mortified, her face flushed with heat, especially when she felt Hart staring at her in astonishment. She turned to him and silently implored him to play along with her.

She didn't want her parents to learn about the threats because they wouldn't be worried about themselves. They would be worried about her, and they already worried too much about her, about if she was taking care of herself, if she was working too much, if she was eating right…

Her father's brow creased with more lines than he already had. Her parents had been well into their forties when they'd finally had the baby they'd wanted for so long. It didn't matter that she was twenty-seven now; Wendy would always be their baby.

Her father had kept the gun grasped in his hand. But with her standing between him and Hart, he'd lowered the barrel. "You were arguing," he said, suspicion in his voice. He wasn't readily accepting her explanation, but then, it was no wonder since Wendy could not even remember the last time she'd had a boyfriend. "I heard raised voices."

"He, uh, surprised me," Wendy said. "Scared me…" That was no lie.

"Of course he did, breaking into our damn house like this!" her father angrily exclaimed. Then he turned his focus on Hart and demanded, "Who the hell are you?"

"Shh, Daddy," Wendy implored him. "You're going to wake up Mom."

And if the police noticed all the lights coming on inside the house, they would probably storm in with more guns drawn.

She glanced down as she realized she wore only that big T-shirt. If the officers saw her like this, she would never hear the end of it around the station. Wendy grabbed a pair of yoga pants and quickly pulled them on.

"Your mother's knee was bothering her, so she took some pain pills," Dad said. "She won't wake up for another six hours."

That was good. At least, if the police stormed inside, her mother wouldn't wake up.

"I'm sorry, sir," Hart said. "I hadn't wanted to disturb either you or your wife."

That much Wendy believed was definitely true. Could she believe the rest of what he'd told her, though? That the chief had hired the Payne Protection to guard the principals in Luther Mills's trial?

It made more sense than his working for Luther. Part of the reason she'd had a crush on him, besides his movie star good looks, was that he'd been such a good cop. He'd made so many arrests.

"I just really needed to see Wendy," he continued. Then he holstered his weapon and held out his hand. "I'm Hart Fisher."

Her father stared at his hand for a long moment. "And how do you know my daughter?"

"We used to work together," Hart replied. "I was a River City detective."

"Oh." Her father nodded. "Of course…"

Had she mentioned Hart to him? She might as well have. She'd told her mother about her crush, and her parents told each other everything. Her face heated even more as her discomfort increased. She tended to share too much with her mother.

Her father extended his hand and heartily shook Hart's. Maybe a little too heartily. Even though he was pushing seventy, her father was a big man, and the former football coach still worked out regularly.

"I'm Ben Thompson." He greeted Hart, but he wasn't smiling.

"I am really sorry," Hart said again. "I just need to speak with Wendy for a few moments, if that's all right with you, sir?"

Her father grunted. "That's not up to me." He looked

at Wendy, really looked at her in that way fathers had that made their children squirm. Or in the way that coaches made their players squirm. "Do you want him to stay, Wendy?"

Now she felt compelled to apologize. "I'm sorry, Dad..."

"You're an adult," her father said.

Sometimes she wondered if he really believed that, though. But he must have been trying to prove that he did because he stepped into the hall and pulled her bedroom door shut—leaving her alone with Hart Fisher. Her bodyguard.

That was what he was. Not her boyfriend.

She didn't want him as either. Not anymore. Now was not the time for her to start dating anyone, not when everyone and everything she cared about had been threatened.

Her face was still so hot that she probably could have melted an ice cube on her forehead.

"I don't want my parents to know about the threats," she explained. "That's why I told my dad that you're my boyfriend." She didn't want Hart to think she wanted that—that she wanted him. Just a short time ago, when he'd been lying on top of her, she'd thought he might have wanted her, too.

But that wasn't possible. He still wouldn't have noticed her if he hadn't been assigned to protect her.

Hart nodded. "I get it," he assured her. "And now I need to get you to that meeting."

She shook her head.

He sighed. "Do you still not trust me, even after I covered for you with your dad?"

If he was working for Luther, he probably would have shot her father instead of apologizing to him. But just because Hart wasn't working for Luther didn't mean she should trust him.

He groaned at her hesitation and reached for his cell. "I'll call the chief—"

"That's not it," she said with a glance at the closed door. "I can't just walk out of here with you in the middle of the night."

Her father was bound to have questions if they left the house now. In fact, she wouldn't be surprised to open her door and find him waiting in the hall outside. She had never been a very good liar, so she was already pushing her luck with all the lies she'd already told.

"We'll go out the way I came in," Hart told her as he headed toward her open window. After slinging one leg over the sill, he held out his hand to her.

Wendy was scared. Not of falling out the window. She'd climbed out that window a time or two in her youth, but not with a boyfriend. Not even to meet a boyfriend. She'd just climbed out to go to movies that had opened after her midnight curfew. She knew it was a short drop from the window to the porch roof below. Then it was an easy climb down the trestle at the end of the porch to the ground.

No. She wasn't scared of falling.

She was scared—of spending too much time with Hart Fisher. She suspected she was in almost as much danger from him as she was from Luther Mills.

* * *

"You've definitely got a problem," Hart told Chief Lynch as he and Wendy joined him in the conference room at the Payne Protection Agency.

The chief arched a gray brow over blue eyes that were bright and alert despite the late hour. "Did something happen at Ms. Thompson's home?"

Besides her not waiting outside for him like he'd thought she would be? Besides his making the risky move of breaking in and nearly getting shot?

Hart shook his head. "But that's the problem. Nobody noticed me sneaking in and out of that house."

"My father did," Wendy chimed in with a slight smile.

Hart shuddered as he remembered the older man throwing open the door and training that gun barrel on him. "It's good that he can protect himself and your mother." He turned back to the chief, who stood at the end of a long conference table. "Because I don't trust that unit you have stationed outside their house to protect them."

The chief flinched.

Hart felt a twinge of regret that he had offended the older man even though Woodrow Lynch shouldn't have been offended. He hadn't had much to do with the existing police force. He hadn't hired or trained them. He'd just recently taken the position of River City police chief after giving up his role as an FBI Bureau chief.

Wendy must have been offended, too, because her elbow jabbed his ribs. Now he felt a twinge of pain— from where her elbow had jabbed him earlier when he'd tried helping her out of the bedroom window. After elbowing him aside, she'd easily slipped over the sill and had moved silently across the roof to the trestle. He'd insisted on going down first, to catch her in case she fell and to make sure nobody could grab her on the ground.

That had been a mistake because, from the ground, all Hart had been able to see was her ass as she'd scrambled down the trestle. She had moved so quickly that she'd slipped. When he'd caught her, his hands cupping her ass, she'd elbowed him again.

That time might have been an accident. This time was definitely not. But Hart wasn't out of line—not with lives at stake.

"Somebody should have noticed us leaving," he insisted. What if he had been one of Luther's crew?

Neither the chief nor Wendy could argue with him now. Lynch sighed. "That's why I brought in Payne Protection."

"Why Parker's team?"

The question came from someone other than Hart. His former coworker Tyce Jackson. The bearded man sat at the table beside Judge Holmes and his daughter, Bella. In the same way Luther had threatened Wendy's family, the threat he'd used to try to influence the judge was that his daughter was in danger. Woodrow Lynch had been right to call in the Payne Protection Agency. Whatever other motives the chief might have had were beside the point.

Lynch answered Tyce. "I figured Parker's team had a vested interest in making sure Luther Mills was finally brought to justice."

Hart winced with regret, frustrated that he hadn't taken down Luther himself. Tyce might have winced, as well, but with as bushy as his black beard was, it was impossible to tell. When they'd worked Vice—with Parker—they'd all tried for years to bring down Luther. But the drug dealer had been too powerful then. Would he prove to be too powerful now?

"Where is Parker?" Hart asked.

Parker had been in his office earlier, but maybe he'd left to look for some of the others. Not everyone was here yet.

Even as he thought that, the door opened. The assistant district attorney, Jocelyn Gerber, walked in, her bodyguard, former vice cop Landon Myers, behind her.

Then the door opened again and Detective Spencer Dubridge entered midargument with his bodyguard, Keeli Abbott. They appeared to be arguing over who should walk first through the door. The detective might have been trying to be a gentleman, but Keeli, the former RCPD cop, would undoubtedly be offended. When they'd all worked together in Vice, the very capable female officer had accused Dubridge of being a male chauvinist.

What the hell had Parker been thinking when he'd made these matchups? Landon and Keeli might not mind if someone harmed the people they were supposed to be protecting.

"Parker was checking on someone in his office," the chief told Hart with a smile. He must have known about Felicity.

Hart's usual babysitter had got sick and had dropped

the little girl off at his work. It was a good thing Parker had been here then and that he was good with kids. The backup sitter should be arriving soon if she hadn't already.

"Then he was going outside to consult with the perimeter guards," Lynch added.

Parker and the chief had been smart to have extra security for this meeting. If Luther Mills had learned about it, the opportunity of having everyone associated with the trial in one place would have been too great for him to pass up.

Since they had no idea who and where his informants were, Mills might have heard about it. He could have ordered a hit...

Hart tilted his head and listened. But he heard no sound of gunfire.

"The eyewitness isn't here," Assistant DA Jocelyn Gerber said, her voice rising with alarm as she looked around the conference room. "Where is she?"

"Parker is checking on that, too," the chief said.

The woman's already pale face lost the little bit of color it had had. "This is bad..."

"This is ridiculous," Wendy said. "We don't need extra protection. Not even Luther Mills can take out everyone associated with his trial."

"He doesn't have to take out everyone," Gerber said. "Just the eyewitness." She focused her pale blue eyes on Wendy and added, "And you."

Because with Wendy gone, it would be difficult to prove that the chain of evidence had remained unbroken. Since she'd collected it from the murder scene, she was the most important link in the chain.

Luther Mills leaned back on the thin mattress in his cell and uttered a sigh. He wouldn't be here much longer. The plan was already starting to work. He'd just been informed that the eyewitness had gone out a window.

Sure, that hadn't exactly been part of the plan. The crew he'd sent after her was supposed to have shot her. But her apartment was on the third floor. A fall from that height had probably killed her and the man they'd said had gone out the window with her. Clint Quarters. What the hell had the former vice cop been doing there?

Had he just been checking on Rosie out of guilt? Quarters was the cop who'd got her brother killed by turning him into an informant. That kind of betrayal deserved the death sentence Luther had given Javier Mendez.

It was too bad Luther had had to deliver that same sentence to Rosie. If only she'd learned the lesson her brother should have… If only she had kept her sexy damn mouth shut…

But her testimony wasn't Luther's only problem. There was all that evidence from the scene, too.

Evidence that shouldn't have been found.

That wouldn't have been found if probably any other crime scene tech had been involved. Everybody knew not to look too closely at a crime he'd committed.

Little Miss By-the-Book Wendy Thompson was as

big a pain in Luther's ass as this damn uncomfortable jailhouse mattress.

But he would get rid of her and the evidence just as easily as he'd got rid of the eyewitness.

Chapter 3

"That's lucky for you," Jocelyn Gerber remarked after Rosie Mendez left the conference room with the chief and Parker Payne, her bodyguard, Clint Quarters, trailing behind them.

Wendy was so tired that she didn't understand what the assistant district attorney was talking about. "What's lucky for me?"

"That the eyewitness is still alive," Jocelyn said.

"She might not stay that way if she keeps fighting having a bodyguard," Hart remarked with a pointed glance at Wendy.

She shivered, but she wasn't scared for her safety, despite how much Hart and the assistant district attorney seemed to be trying to scare her. She was probably just cold. A thin T-shirt wasn't enough protection against the chill of the late autumn evening.

And maybe she was a little chilled from the threats, as well. Needing backup, she looked down the conference table at Spencer Dubridge. "Don't you think this is ridiculous, too?" she asked the detective who had had the pleasure of arresting Luther Mills. "We can protect ourselves."

He glanced sideways at his female bodyguard and snorted. "I certainly can protect myself better than Bodyguard Barbie can protect me."

Keeli Abbott glared at him and Wendy suspected Dubridge's former coworker might be from whom the detective most needed to protect himself.

The conference room door opened and the chief stepped back inside. As if he'd overheard their conversation, he insisted, "Everyone is going to have a bodyguard—" he stared hard at Dubridge "—no matter who they are, until this trial is over and Luther Mills is sentenced to life behind bars."

Judge Holmes shook his head. "I can't be party to this conversation."

"You didn't need to be here," the chief told him. "Your daughter is the one being threatened." Bella Holmes was not a minor; she had to be at least midtwenties.

"And she wouldn't leave her damn party until her father told her she had to," Tyce Jackson grumbled through his bushy beard. Even though he didn't work Vice anymore, he still looked like he had when he'd gone deep undercover.

Hart must have never worked undercover because

he'd always been clean-shaved and well-groomed. That was why Wendy had had such a crush on him. He'd always looked so handsome.

Bella Holmes glared at Tyce. "I didn't know who you were." Maybe she'd judged him by the way he looked.

Tyce had been one of those vice cops who'd gone so deeply undercover that sometimes it was difficult to return to the life they'd once lived. Wendy suspected that was the case with him.

"If you'd listened to your dad's message, you wouldn't have been at that damn party," Tyce griped.

So Wendy wasn't the only one who hadn't played a voice mail that she'd needed to hear. She didn't feel any better about the situation, though. If she'd listened, she could have spared her dad a surprise and herself having to lie to him again.

"We are not going to stop living our lives just because of these threats," Wendy reminded the chief. "So how do we explain having bodyguards? How is the rest of the precinct going to feel that you didn't trust our fellow officers to protect me or Detective Dubridge or even Ms. Gerber?"

"You told your father that I'm your boyfriend," Hart reminded her. "Maybe we just tell everyone else the same damn thing."

Heat rushed to her face again, chasing away that chill she'd briefly felt.

Dubridge chuckled. "That'll work for her. Everybody in the department knows she had a crush on Fisher even back when he was married."

Wendy gasped in shock that everyone else had known about the crush she'd shared with only a few close coworkers. Maybe Hart was right. She couldn't trust them.

The detective blithely continued. "But that won't work for everyone else."

The judge's daughter glanced sideways at Tyce and nodded. "I should say not…"

"You're not my type, either," Tyce assured her, his voice so deep it was just a rumble.

"And chauvinist pig is certainly not mine," Keeli Abbott remarked.

The chief groaned. His voice rising with frustration, he yelled, "You're all supposed to be professionals here. Figure it out!"

"Professional partier maybe," Tyce Jackson murmured with a glance at Bella Holmes.

She glared at him again.

Wendy didn't even dare to glance at Hart. What did he think of her? He probably pitied her if he had heard the rumors like Dubridge had. Did he know she'd had a crush on him even when he was married—like some adolescent girl with a crush on a teen idol?

Still arguing, everyone else filed out of the conference room, leaving Wendy and Hart alone. Even the chief had stepped out, deep in conversation with Jocelyn Gerber. But then the door opened again.

Maybe he had returned.

But it wasn't the chief who had walked through the door; a tiny little blonde girl barreled into the room.

"Daddy!" she squealed. "Mr. Parker said you were back." She jumped onto Hart's lap.

He closed his arms around her. "You're supposed to be sleeping," he admonished. But the rebuke was gentle, as were his warm brown eyes as he stared lovingly at her.

Hart Fisher had a child?

How had Wendy never heard that?

The little girl noticed Wendy and shyly buried her face in the doll she grasped in her delicate-looking arms. Then she suddenly pulled the doll away from her face and held it up near Wendy's. Her blue eyes widened with shock as she looked from Wendy to the stuffed doll and then back at Wendy.

"She looks like my dolly, Daddy," she murmured, her voice soft with awe. "She looks like Annie."

Wendy felt her face heat all over again with embarrassment. First, she was outed for crushing on her bodyguard like a schoolgirl. Now she was being compared to a rag doll.

Her ego had taken a hell of a beating—far more painful than anything Luther Mills or his crew could have doled out to her.

"My dolly's name is Annie," the little girl told her. "What's your name?"

"Wendy," she replied. An only child who'd grown up around the teenage football players her father had coached, Wendy wasn't comfortable around little girls. Despite her mother's best efforts by forcing pink and frills on her, Wendy had never been a little girl herself. She had always been, and probably still was, a tomboy.

"Winnie," the little girl repeated—incorrectly.

Wendy didn't correct her. She just asked, "And what is your name?"

"Felicity…" she said slowly, as if she struggled to pronounce her own name. It was quite the mouthful.

"That's pretty," Wendy said.

"You're pretty," the little girl said with that slow, shy smile.

Something wrapped around Wendy's heart, tightly squeezing it. Felicity's mother was reputedly a former beauty queen. Why in the world would the child think Wendy was pretty?

She was obviously just a very sweet girl.

"You are the pretty one," Wendy said. Felicity looked like a doll, but the kind made of porcelain and kept behind glass—delicate and beautiful—not one made with burlap and bright red yarn.

The little girl scrambled off her father's lap and climbed onto Wendy's. She held out her doll for Wendy to admire. "Grandma made me this doll when I was borned," she said. "Now Grandma is an angel."

That grasp on Wendy's heart tightened even more. "I'm sorry, honey," she murmured.

"Why?" the little girl asked. She reached out and fingered a lock of Wendy's curly hair. But her touch was tentative as though she thought it would be hot since it was so red. Wendy smiled reassuringly at her, and the little girl smiled back.

"People say that when they find out you've lost someone you love," Hart explained to his daughter.

Wendy hoped nobody would have cause to say that

to her. She could not lose her parents. Luther was just trying to scare her into destroying the evidence. Right? He wouldn't actually harm them...

But then she remembered how the eyewitness and her bodyguard had looked when they'd joined the meeting earlier. They had gone out a window, too, but not like she and Hart had. No, Rosie and Clint had been forced to jump to avoid being shot to death.

She shivered and the little girl snuggled a little closer to her. Her long black lashes fluttered as her eyelids began to droop. She murmured to her father, "I'm sorry, Daddy..."

He touched his daughter's cheek, which was uncomfortably close to Wendy's breast. She tensed and drew in a shaky breath. But he didn't touch her. He was focused only on his daughter.

"Why are you sorry, baby?" he asked. The love Wendy had seen in his eyes was in his voice now.

"For you, Daddy," she murmured sleepily. "You've lost a lot of people you love."

Her mother? Had he loved and lost her?

Not that Wendy cared. She didn't care about anything but keeping her family safe. But she didn't want Hart's family to be in danger, either. She tightened her arm around the little girl and leaned close enough that her chin brushed the soft blond hair, asking him, "So is this Bring Your Daughter to Work day?"

His face flushed with a bit of color. "A babysitter should be showing up soon."

"It's a weeknight," she said.

He nodded. "Yes, and she's just turned four. She's not in school yet."

"But why do you have her now?" she asked.

His brow furrowed for a moment then cleared. "You think I'm just a weekend father?" He shook his head. "I have full custody."

While she had no personal experience with it, Wendy had several divorced friends and acquaintances, especially since law enforcement was so hard on relationships.

The long hours officers worked...

The things they saw...

They all took their toll.

And usually because of those long hours, they weren't granted much more than weekend visitations. But maybe that was why Hart had resigned from the police department. For his daughter...

Then why had he taken another dangerous job with long hours?

She wasn't going to be responsible for taking him away from his child. Over the little girl's head, she met Hart's gaze and told him, "You can't be my bodyguard."

"I don't want to be your bodyguard," Hart admitted. He hadn't been certain if his coworkers had been telling the truth or just teasing him about that crush, but he hadn't wanted to take the chance that it was the truth and Wendy got her feelings hurt.

And she would get hurt if she made the mistake of falling for him. His ability to trust and love were gone.

Long gone...

He had nothing left to give anyone but Felicity.

Wendy expelled a shaky breath that stirred Felicity's hair. But the little girl didn't move. She'd fallen fast asleep in the arms of a stranger.

Hart couldn't believe how his daughter had taken to Wendy Thompson. Felicity was always so shy, but never more so than around women. Her mother hadn't ever been very patient with her. Monica never would have allowed Felicity to touch her hair. She would have been afraid the child would mess it up or make it sticky.

But Wendy hadn't cared. As if she'd sensed the child's fear, she had smiled reassuringly at her. And Hart had felt a strange twinge in his chest—one that he felt again just staring at the two of them.

"Good," she said. "Tell Parker that you can't."

"Already did," he informed her. "But he refused. Said he had no one else to give the assignment to." All the other team members had already been assigned someone to protect. Hart suspected Parker, like everyone else in the RCPD, had heard the rumors about Wendy's crush. Now that crush could be used to explain his presence in her life; they could claim he was her boyfriend—just as she had already told her father.

She shook her head. "I don't need a bodyguard," she said. "I'll be fine."

"Didn't you hear what the assistant DA said?" he asked. Frustration with her stubbornness had him raising his voice. But when Felicity stirred against her, he lowered it when he continued. "For Luther to get off, the eyewitness isn't the only one he needs to take out."

Wendy tightened her arm around his daughter and

lowered her voice to a whisper. "He doesn't need to take *me* out. Just the evidence."

Hart nodded. "That's true. I'm sure he could get to anyone else in your department to get it thrown out." He would either pay them or threaten them.

Neither of those options would work on someone like Wendy, though. On someone so stubborn.

Her face flushed with indignation, turning nearly as red as her hair. "He can't *get* to *anyone* else in my department," she protested. "He does not have an evidence tech on his payroll."

Hart snorted at her naivete. "Then how have all his previous cases got thrown out?" Luther damn well did have someone working for him. Hell, he had a lot of someones working for him.

So nobody could be trusted.

"I don't know about the evidence in his previous cases," Wendy said, "but I know nobody's getting to this evidence but me."

He narrowed his eyes as he studied her face. "You've hidden it somewhere?"

"That prior evidence disappeared from the evidence room," she said.

"So this evidence is not there?" he asked.

She shook her head. "It's somewhere safe that won't compromise the chain of evidence."

Maybe she wasn't as naive as he'd thought. "Obviously you don't trust your coworkers as much as you claim you do."

"If anyone else knew where it was, they would be

threatened, too," she said, "and I don't want to put anybody else in danger."

Now he understood why she'd said what she had. "That's why you don't want me as your bodyguard. You don't want me in danger."

Her face reddened even more. "Don't think it's because of some nonexistent crush I supposedly have on you," she said, sputtering. She lowered her green-eyed gaze from his and stared down at his daughter. "It's because of her."

That twinge struck Hart's chest again.

"She needs you," Wendy said. "I don't."

He flinched. But he couldn't argue with her about Felicity. His daughter did need him. She really had no one else. Not now. Not since Hart's mother had passed away a couple of years ago. She had been the only maternal figure his little girl had ever known when her own mother had failed to ever show any interest in her. After she'd had her, Monica had admitted to only getting pregnant so Hart wouldn't divorce her. Abandoned as a child, she'd been determined that nobody else leave her; she was always the one who left. Unfortunately, she hadn't left just him but their daughter, as well.

"Felicity's not going to lose me," Hart said. He hoped his daughter knew that. "I'm not leaving her. I'm just doing my job. And I'm damn good at my job." He'd been a good vice cop and then a detective, so being a bodyguard had come very naturally to him. "Nothing's going to happen to me."

But he wondered if he was really telling the truth.

He wasn't worried about being physically hurt, though. He was worried about becoming too entangled with Wendy Thompson—like he had in her bed when he'd first sneaked through her window and had tried to keep her quiet. He was also worried about Wendy Thompson becoming too entangled with him and his daughter.

No. Felicity couldn't lose anyone else. So his little girl could not get attached to Wendy—because Hart was only going to pretend to be the evidence tech's boyfriend. He had no intention of ever being involved with anyone ever again.

All that type of involvement led to was betrayal and emotional pain. And that was the kind of pain he wasn't going to risk experiencing ever again. He'd much rather risk his life than his heart.

Even though he was in jail, there was no escaping Luther Mills. Once he got hold of someone, he didn't let go and he didn't let up. One could not say no to Luther—not and live.

Wendy Thompson was so young and naive that she had not yet realized that.

But she would. Soon.

The person crawled under the vehicle parked in the driveway of Thompson's parents' house. Hands, in leather gloves, located the brake line. Then a knife cut neatly through the line, spilling fluid onto the asphalt.

By morning all the fluid would have leaked out. Maybe then Wendy would finally get the message all those threats had tried to deliver to her.

The evidence needed to disappear or, just as the messages had warned, everything and everyone Wendy Thompson held dear would disappear instead.

Chapter 4

Her heart pounding fast and hard, Wendy closed the front door of her parents' house behind her. She leaned back against the solid wood for a moment to catch a breath of fresh air. She felt as if she'd just run the gauntlet, trying to escape the shots fired at her. Those shots hadn't been bullets, though—just questions her parents had asked her this morning.

They had had so many of them.

"How long have you and Hart been dating?"

"Why didn't you tell us?"

"How serious are you?"

"What was so important that he had to see you in the middle of the night?"

Their lives. That was what was so important. In addition to the police car stationed in the area, the Payne

Protection Agency had assigned bodyguards to them, as well. But they would not see the bodyguards.

Wendy couldn't see them, either, when she looked around the house and street as she walked to the car parked on the driveway. Where were they?

The bodyguards weren't from Parker's team but one of his brother's. She'd asked if one of them could protect her instead of Hart. But just as Hart had warned her, Parker had refused to assign her a different bodyguard. And Chief Lynch had backed him up.

Of course everyone thought Hart should protect her. They'd known about her crush on him and, because of that, they'd believed everyone would buy that he was her boyfriend. Heat rushed to her face with humiliation that her attraction to the former detective was such common knowledge. But Hart had never showed any interest in her. That had to be common knowledge, as well.

So would anyone actually believe that he was her boyfriend? That he'd suddenly noticed her now—when he hadn't noticed her all the years they'd worked together even after his divorce?

Her parents had been suspicious. Or they wouldn't have fired so many questions at her.

Those questions had been hard to dodge because lying to her parents had never been easy. But in this case, it had been necessary. She didn't want to worry them.

Like she was worried.

They would be safe, with the police watching them, with Payne Protection bodyguards watching them.

Luther wouldn't be able to get to them now—not

with so many people protecting them. But if the threats continued, she would tell them; she would urge them to leave town for their safety and hers. She would be more careful herself if she didn't have to worry about them, as well.

She clicked the fob to unlock the car, but before she could pull open the driver's door, a deep voice murmured, "Good morning."

She jumped even though she instantly recognized that voice. When she turned to face him, Hart Fisher was very close. So close that their bodies brushed against each other.

Her pulse quickened with excitement, not fear, with the attraction she felt for him—that she had always felt for him. But she didn't want him to know that she had really had a crush on him. She already felt foolish enough about it.

"What the hell are you doing?" she asked as she glanced nervously around.

The curtains swished at the front window of her parents' house. Someone was watching them.

"I'm trying to do my damn job," Hart said through gritted teeth as he very obviously faked a grin.

When he'd dropped her off last night, she had refused to let him inside the house. From the dark circles beneath his eyes, he must not have slept at all. Too bad his daughter's babysitter had arrived at the agency before they'd left. He wouldn't have been able to take Wendy home if he'd had to take care of Felicity.

But even though his babysitter had shown up, the

little girl still needed her father—especially since he had full custody. Where was her mother?

"You need a safer job," she told him.

"I'm fine," he said, but his voice lowered even more to a growl of frustration. "It's my assignment that's a pain in the ass."

She smiled—just as artificially as he had. "Then you need another assignment."

He shook his head. "This is the one I have," he said. "So I'm going to make the best of it."

Then he did something she hadn't expected. He lowered his head until his mouth brushed across hers.

Her pulse began to race and she gasped.

He kissed her again, lingering this time—his lips clinging to hers before he deepened the kiss even more. When he finally lifted his head, she gasped again—this time for breath.

"What the hell was that?" she asked.

He arched his head toward the front window of the house. "For our audience."

"You're overacting," she said because she had to remind herself that was all he was doing. Acting...

He wasn't really her boyfriend. He wasn't really attracted to her. He was only pretending.

Yet the kiss had felt real to her, so real that desire coursed through her. She wanted him. But he only wanted to do his job.

She had a job of her own to do, though. "You're going to make me late," she said. "I need to get to work."

"Then get in my SUV," he said. "And I will take you to work."

She shook her head. "I need to have my own vehicle." But her vehicle was actually in a service shop right now. Since her mother hadn't been cleared to drive yet with her new right knee, Wendy was using her mom's car.

With obvious skepticism, Hart narrowed his eyes. "If you have to go out to a crime scene, you use the department van to collect evidence," he said.

"Yes, and you can't go with me if I'm called to a crime scene," she said.

He lifted his broad shoulders. "I can't ride in the van," he said. "But I have every intention of following you."

"You're not going to look like my boyfriend. You're going to look like a stalker," she said.

He grinned and leaned closer. So close that his lips brushed lightly across hers again. "Or like a man in love…who suspects a killer might be threatening his girlfriend."

Her heart skipped a beat until he shuddered as if the idea repulsed him. The idea of being her boyfriend? Or of a killer being after her?

While she curved her lips into a smile, she glared at him and pushed him back so she could pull open the driver's door. "Since you apparently intend to follow me to crime scenes, you can follow me to the station," she said. "Because I'm driving myself there."

Before he could reach for her again, she slid into the seat and jammed the key into the ignition. He cursed, or started to, but she turned the key and the engine drowned him out. He stepped back as she reversed the car into the street.

She shifted into Drive and pressed hard on the accelerator. Since he wasn't going to make it easy for her to do her job, she wasn't going to make it easy for him to do his. She intended to be long gone before he could even get to his SUV.

But speeding in a residential area wasn't smart. So she reached for the brake pedal, pressing lightly on it. But the car didn't slow. At all...

She pressed harder until the pedal went all the way to the floor. Nothing happened.

The car would not stop. The brakes had gone out. And since her father almost fanatically maintained his vehicles, Wendy knew they hadn't gone out on their own. Someone had cut the brake line.

She could not stop.

Hart shook his head, disgusted with himself that he'd just let her drive off. But with her parents watching, there was little more he could have done to stop her, especially since he knew her father was armed. Even now he had to force himself not to run to his SUV. He had to keep the smile on his face until he turned away from the house. But then he glanced down at the driveway and his heart slammed against his ribs as he noticed fluid pooled on the asphalt where her car had been parked.

He didn't have to dip his finger in it to know where the fluid had come from. Her brake line.

He could hear the squeal of tires against asphalt.

A horn blew.

He knew she was already unable to stop.

He ran, jumping into his SUV. His hand shook as he turned the key, fired the engine to life and roared out of the driveway after her.

But she already had quite a head start on him. And she couldn't slow down.

Fortunately, it was so early that there wasn't much traffic yet, and the SUV had a bigger engine than her little sedan. He was able to speed enough that he caught up with her.

Despite not having brakes, she managed to steer around a corner. The street onto which she'd turned had fewer houses. But it went downhill, so she was gaining speed.

And she had no way to stop.

Hart would have to stop her before the car went even faster. Or she would die for certain.

He pressed harder on his accelerator and crossed over the center line so that he was next to her. She glanced out her window at him. Her eyes were wide with fear, her face so pale that her freckles stood out even more than usual.

She gripped the wheel tightly.

He gestured at the gearshift. If she could get the vehicle into Neutral…

He clicked the power button to lower his passenger-side window.

She lowered her window. "I have no brakes!" she yelled.

"Neutral," he yelled back at her.

But the loud blare of a horn might have drowned out

his command. Just a short distance ahead of them, a semitruck had backed out of a driveway and was blocking the street. If she hit it head-on, she was certain to die.

So he jerked his wheel and smashed into the side of her car. Metal ground against metal, screeching as it scraped together.

Maybe it wasn't just the screeching metal he heard. Maybe it was Wendy screaming because her mouth was open as she stared at him in shock.

He'd had no choice, though. He had to get her off the road and out of the path of that truck. He wrenched the wheel even harder, crunching the side of her car as he pushed it off the road.

Her tires hit the curb before the car jumped the sidewalk. He breathed a sigh of relief that she was off the street, until he saw where she was heading—straight toward a tree.

A massive oak with a trunk wider than her little car. He swerved over the curb, too, trying to get between her and the tree. But he was too late.

Her car struck the trunk of the oak, wrapping itself around it. Another horn blared—this one was hers as her body slumped against the airbag that had exploded from her steering wheel.

Had he saved her?

Or killed her?

"What the hell did you say?" Parker exclaimed. Then he pulled his cell phone away from his ear and stared at it.

He could not have heard his sister correctly. Nikki

was one of the guards he'd posted outside Wendy Thompson's parents' house; he'd borrowed her from his brother Cooper's team. Maybe their cell connection was faulty.

"What happened?" he asked, seeking clarification.

"I don't know," Nikki replied. "First they were kissing…"

Parker groaned. "No…"

Hart was only supposed to pretend to be her boyfriend. They weren't supposed to really become involved. Of all his bodyguards, Parker had thought Hart, who'd barely survived his short marriage, was immune to the temptation of mixing pleasure with business.

Sure, he was aware that Wendy Thompson had had a crush on Hart when he'd worked for River City PD, and while that was useful for their cover, Parker had never expected either of them to actually act on it.

"The kissing might have been for her parents' benefit," Nikki speculated. "They were not very discreetly watching them through the front window."

His heart thudded heavily with dread. "So did they see what you just told me happened?" He was still hoping that he'd misunderstood. That she couldn't have said what she had…

But then Nikki repeated it. "Him running her off the road?"

Parker groaned again. So he had heard his sister correctly the first time.

"They couldn't have seen it," Nikki said. "It happened a couple of miles from their house. Lars is still sitting on their place and the Thompsons haven't made any attempt to leave. They must have not even heard the crash."

Crash. Parker flinched.

"I don't understand," he said. "How did they get from kissing to separate vehicles and…?"

What? A road rage incident?

"After the kissing, she jumped in her car and took off," Nikki told him.

To do what? Report Hart to him or to the chief? This was bad. Very bad.

"It didn't take long to figure out, from the way she was driving, that her brakes must have gone out," Nikki said. "Hart was right there. I think he tried to force her off the road so she wouldn't hit the truck. But…"

"But what?" Parker asked.

"She hit a tree instead."

Parker shot up from his desk and cursed. "Oh, my God. Is she okay?"

"I don't know," Nikki said. "I radioed Hart and he claims he's got it handled." But she obviously doubted his abilities. She didn't know Hart Fisher like Parker did, though.

"If Hart says he's got it handled, he does." Parker wasn't sure if he backed his friend out of loyalty, though, or because he actually believed what he was saying. Hart Fisher had been a good cop—so good that he'd made detective right before he'd quit the force.

Since Parker had hired him, he'd proved to be a damn good bodyguard, too.

Until today.

Today, instead of protecting his principal, he might have put her in more danger.

Chapter 5

The metal was so twisted and bent, Wendy had to move carefully beneath it so that no sharp edges cut her. Fluids dripped onto the grass and her face and clothes. She suspected it was antifreeze and transmission fluid. The brake fluid was gone. When she located the line, she saw why; it had been neatly sliced straight through.

She sucked in some air, happy that she could breathe again after the airbag had knocked the breath out of her. It had also saved her life, though. Once the rush of adrenaline left her, she would be sore and have some bumps and bruises, but other than that, she was going to be fine.

She needed to get the car into the police garage and up on a hoist, so she could take pictures of the damage. After she'd done that, she would be able to remove the line to see if she could figure out what kind of tool had cut it so cleanly. A knife? Switchblade? Razor?

She peered closer, trying to figure it out. But before she could discern what might have been used to cut it, strong fingers wrapped tightly around her ankles and dragged her out from beneath the wreckage.

"What the hell are you doing?" she asked as she stared up at Hart's face.

His chiseled features twisted into a grimace while his skin flushed with anger. "What the hell are *you* doing?" he demanded.

"Processing evidence," she replied matter-of-factly even as her heart continued to pound so quickly and heavily. "Someone deliberately cut the brake line."

"You could have been killed," he said, his deep voice cracking with anger.

She was angry, too, but she found herself turning that anger on him. "Yes, thanks to you, I nearly was."

"Thanks to me?" he sputtered.

"You ran me off the road!" She gestured at the tree and was surprised to see how badly her hand was shaking now.

Why was she shaking so? It was all over. She was fine. It must have just been the adrenaline that continued to rush through her.

He shook his head in denial.

"Was it someone else? It sure as hell looked like you behind the wheel," she said.

"I didn't want you to hit that semitruck," he said.

She knew that; knew that he had probably saved her life and that she should be thanking him. But she feared that if she let the anger go, she would fall apart. And because she didn't know yet who had cut her brake line, she vented her anger on Hart.

"That tree is nearly as big as the truck!" she said.

He flinched. "I didn't see the tree."

Neither had she. But she hadn't hit it head-on like she would have the truck. The passenger's side and front corner of her mother's car had taken the brunt of the impact. The airbag had protected her from any serious harm.

She was going to be a little sore from the force of the collision. But she was only alive because of Hart. If not for Hart…

She shuddered as she realized that she had nearly died. And she started shaking even more than she had been.

"I told you to put it in Neutral," he said. "Didn't you hear me?"

"I did," she said. "And I did. But there was just too much momentum." The car wouldn't have stopped until it had hit something or someone.

Hart hadn't just saved her life but probably other lives, as well. She had yet to thank him. Shame heated her face. She opened her mouth to apologize, but before she could say anything, he interrupted her.

"I'm sorry," Hart said, offering the apology first. "Are you okay?"

He'd asked that the minute he'd run up to her car. But instead of answering him, she'd pushed open the driver's door and scrambled under the wreckage.

Emotions overwhelmed her, nearly choking her, so

all she could manage was a brief nod. Since becoming an evidence tech, she had investigated many crime scenes where a murder had taken place. But she had never considered before that her life might one day become a crime scene—and the murder hers.

Luther Mills wasn't just threatening her anymore. He was making good on those threats. He intended to kill her.

What about her parents?

"Oh, my God," she murmured when what had really just happened finally sank in. She began to tremble even more as fear rushed over her.

Hart reached out for Wendy, grasping her shoulders so that she didn't fall over. Her face had gone so pale, her brilliant green eyes so wide with horror. She must have gone into shock. Maybe she'd been in shock since her car had crashed into the tree, and she hadn't even noticed how injured she actually was. She could have internal bleeding, a concussion…

"We need to get you to the hospital," he said. He should have taken her to the ER the moment she'd extricated herself from the wreckage. But she hadn't given him the chance before she'd tried collecting evidence. "You need to have X-rays and find out the extent of your injuries."

She shook her head again and pulled free of his loose grasp. "I need to call for a tow truck to get this car into the police garage."

"You can't process your own car for evidence," Hart told her, especially not when she was hurt.

"It's not my car," Wendy said, and her voice cracked with fear. "It's my mom's car."

Hart sucked in a sharp breath. Though his mother had passed away a couple of years ago, he still missed her every day. So he understood her emotional reaction. "We'll get that truck here ASAP," he assured her, pulling out his cell phone. "We'll figure out who cut that brake line."

"That's my job," a deep voice murmured.

Hart drew his weapon and pointed his barrel in the direction of the voice. When Spencer Dubridge walked around the front of Hart's SUV, he didn't holster his weapon—not right away.

"I didn't call the police," Hart said. "What the hell are you doing here?"

Spencer shivered as if Hart's attitude chilled him. They'd once been friends—when they'd worked Vice together. Well, they'd been friendly rivals. Certainly more friendly than Spencer was with Keeli Abbott, his bodyguard, who followed him around the SUV.

Hart holstered his weapon.

"The truck driver you nearly hit called it in," Keeli answered for Spencer. "The call came over the radio, and we were close."

"You're not a cop anymore," Spencer told her. He turned back to Hart. "Neither of you are. So this is *my* case."

Keeli snorted her disgust. "He hasn't changed a bit, has he?" she asked Hart. "He's still stealing cases from everybody else."

Spencer shook his head. "*Solving* cases," he corrected her. "Not stealing. And as I just stated, neither of you is with the force anymore. You're quitters."

Keeli recoiled as if he'd slapped her.

Hart couldn't argue with the detective. He had quit the force. But he'd had a very good reason: Felicity.

He suspected Keeli's reason for quitting might have been Dubridge and the chauvinism she'd battled from others like him within the River City Police Department.

"You all gave up on catching Mills," Spencer continued. "I didn't. The arrest was mine."

"The arrest belongs to Clint Quarters," Keeli said. "It was his informant who Luther killed."

That was why Clint had quit the force. Now he was protecting the informant's sister, Rosie Mendez, the eyewitness. Hart didn't envy his friend that assignment. It wasn't going to be easy for many reasons.

But while Hart hadn't wanted to protect Wendy, he hadn't expected the assignment to be this hard, either. He'd been worried that she might fall for him. He hadn't expected Wendy to affect him like she had.

Like that kiss had…

She finally spoke to the others as she reminded them all, "We have to make certain that Mills does not get away with that poor kid's murder." She shuddered as if she was reliving the horror of seeing that all over again.

Since she was the evidence tech, she'd processed the crime scene, which would have included Javier Mendez's bullet-ridden body.

Hart wanted to pull her into his arms again, as if he could protect her from the past as well as the present.

Hell, he knew there was no protection from the past. There were too many things that still haunted him.

"We can't let Mills get away with trying to kill you, either," Spencer added. There was something almost like affection on the detective's face when he looked at her.

Wendy had always been the most requested evidence tech around the station. She did her job very well. She found prints and DNA no one else could find. She was that good.

But Hart wondered if there had ever been anything else between Dubridge and Wendy. Anything personal...

Sure, everybody, including Dubridge, said she'd had a crush on Hart. But that didn't mean another coworker hadn't had a crush on her.

"We don't know yet that it was Luther behind this," she cautioned the detective. "We need to process the evidence first."

"Nobody does that better than you do," Spencer proclaimed, praising her.

Even Keeli's blue eyes widened with surprise at the detective's compliment. Hart had listened to her complain for years that Spencer was a total male chauvinist pig. And around her, he had always seemed to be.

"But you can't process this evidence," Spencer told Wendy. He stepped closer to her and touched her cheek. "And you should get checked out at the hospital."

Something curled low in Hart's stomach, like a snake getting ready to strike. He wanted to slap Dubridge's hand away from her face. He didn't have the right to touch her.

But, hell, Spencer might have more of a right than Hart did, though—if there was something actually going on between the detective and the evidence tech.

"Your bodyguard doesn't seem to be doing a very good job of protecting you." Dubridge goaded him. "Oh, I forgot…he's your *boyfriend* now."

During the meeting at the Payne Protection Agency, Spencer had been the one who'd brought up Wendy's crush on Hart. Was he jealous?

Hart stepped closer to Wendy and slid his arm around her shoulders. But she ducked away from him, as if his touch repulsed her. She hadn't pulled away from his kiss earlier—at least, not right away. But then she hadn't just pulled away from him; she'd jumped in a car and sped away from him. In a car with no brakes…

No. He couldn't argue with Dubridge. He hadn't done a very damn good job of protecting her.

"He's not my boyfriend," Wendy protested. She gestured at Keeli. "Not any more than she's your girlfriend."

Why did she want to make that so clear? Had she replaced her crush on Hart with a crush on Spencer Dubridge? One that he returned?

The detective chuckled as if the thought of his dating Keeli was laughable. And his bodyguard's face flushed bright red with fury.

Hart didn't envy Keeli her assignment.

"We're your personal protection," Keeli said with a ragged sigh. "Let us do our damn jobs."

Dubridge shrugged. "If you want to follow me around like a lovesick puppy, that's up to you." He dropped to the ground to peer under the wrecked car.

"I am not a quitter," Keeli murmured between gritted teeth as if repeating a mantra to herself.

Hart had quit a few things—like the police force and his farce of a marriage. But he was not quitting this job. He was damn well not going to let anything happen to Wendy or to her family. It wasn't because he cared about her or anything. Like she'd said, he wasn't her boyfriend. He was just her bodyguard—with a difficult job to do.

A week had passed since Woodrow Lynch had called that meeting at Payne Protection. He leaned back in his chair and closed his eyes, uttering a weary sigh. It had been an eventful week. So many attempts had been made on the life of the eyewitness.

Hopefully, Rosie Mendez was safe now.

But with her stashed where she couldn't be found, Luther Mills would turn his attention to the other people involved in his prosecution.

A knock at his door compelled the chief to open his eyes. He didn't need his wife's notorious sixth sense to know that the person standing outside his door was now the one in the most danger.

He gestured for Wendy Thompson to come inside.

She opened and closed the door behind her. "I'm glad you finally found the time to meet with me," she said.

A grin tugged at his lips. He had been avoiding her. He hadn't needed to meet with her to know what she wanted—what the witness had wanted, what every damn individual he'd hired personal protection for wanted: to lose his or her bodyguard. But more than anyone else, the evidence tech needed the extra security.

Especially now.

"Why have you wanted to see me?" he asked.

"I don't need a bodyguard following me everywhere," she said and, as she said it, glanced over her shoulder as if worried he had followed her inside the chief's office. She stiffened as she caught sight of Hart Fisher standing on the other side of the big window that looked over the rows of desks for the detectives.

That grin tugged harder at Woodrow's mouth, but he refrained from letting it slip.

A little groan slipped through Wendy's lips, though. "It's ridiculous," she said. "I'm perfectly safe."

"The brake line on your car was cut," the chief reminded her.

"My *mother's* car," she corrected him. "Luther is threatening my parents so I'll destroy the evidence for him. I can't do that if I'm dead, so I can't imagine that he really wants to kill me."

For someone who had worked with the police department as long as she had, processing gruesome crime scenes no less, she was still a bit naive. While it wasn't necessarily a bad thing that the job hadn't got to her yet, it wasn't necessarily good that she was still so trusting—especially with as much danger as she was in.

"I'm not so sure you're right about that," he cautioned her.

"But what does killing me accomplish?" she asked. "It doesn't destroy the evidence."

"No. But it would allow someone else to get to it who would," he pointed out.

She tensed. "Are you suggesting another evidence tech might be working for Luther?"

It would make sense as to why so many other cases against Mills had fallen apart before even making it to the grand jury.

"I'm not suggesting anything," he said. "But I'm allowing for the possibility."

Wendy shook her head. "No. Nobody from my department could be working for him. Nobody in the police department could. The leak must be in the district attorney's office."

"I admire your loyalty to your coworkers," he said. "But you must not have heard the news."

"News?" She tensed and stared at him. "What? What happened?" She glanced through the window at Hart, as if to make sure he was okay.

Maybe she had another reason for wanting to get rid of her bodyguard. Maybe she was getting too attached.

"There was just another attempt on the eyewitness's life."

"Is she okay?" Wendy asked.

Woodrow nodded. "Her bodyguard saved her life and killed the shooter."

"I'm sure that the police would have—had they been protecting her," she asserted.

He shook his head, that weariness making his neck and shoulders ache with tension. "It was a police officer who tried to kill her."

She released a shuddery breath. "Then that's it. It's over. The leak in the department is dead."

He shook his head again. "He couldn't have been acting alone."

"Why not?"

"For one, the information Luther got hold of…"

Mills had a bigger connection than some rookie cop—someone who'd been around the department for a while. Certainly longer than Woodrow had been.

He'd only recently taken over as chief. But he'd thought the department had been cleaned up. One of his former FBI agents had spent years working on flushing out the corrupt officers. He obviously hadn't found them all.

"And for another," he continued, "how did someone so easily get past that police car I had stationed on your parents' house?"

She grimaced slightly and said, "Hart is good at what he does. That's how he got past them."

"I'm not talking about Hart," he said. "I'm talking about whoever sliced that brake line. How did they walk right past that patrol car?"

She shivered as his words and the severity of her situation must have finally sunk in. She needed to be aware, though—to stay alive.

"You can't trust anyone, Ms. Thompson," he cautioned her.

"Then I can't trust Hart Fisher, either," she stubbornly maintained.

He studied the former vice cop through the glass of the window in the wall of his office. Hart Fisher's record as a police officer and detective had been exemplary. It was unfortunate for Woodrow and River City PD that they had lost him.

"I trust Parker Payne," he said. "I trust that he chose his team wisely. Clint Quarters saved Rosie Mendez and she's accepted that he's going to keep her safe until the trial. You need to do the same with Hart Fisher, especially now."

Her green eyes widened in surprise. "Why especially now?"

"Because, with the eyewitness out of his reach, Luther's going to come after you hard," he warned her, "with everything he's got."

The infamous drug lord had already proved that he had a lot of gun power and manpower. Now Woodrow worried that Hart Fisher and the Payne Protection Agency, as good as they were, might not be enough to keep Wendy Thompson alive.

Chapter 6

Hart couldn't see her face, except for those few times she'd glanced at him, but he knew, from the stiffening of her back and shoulders, that the chief wasn't saying anything she wanted to hear. He had a pretty good idea what she'd wanted to hear—that she no longer needed a bodyguard.

But Parker had just called and brought him up to speed on the latest development with the eyewitness and Clint Quarters. Sometime during that call Wendy had slipped out of the evidence lab and sneaked away from him.

She hadn't got far before he'd found her, though. Unfortunately, this was not the first time this week she'd tried giving him the slip. When she drove to crime scenes, she drove the evidence van like she'd driven her mother's car—as if it had no brakes.

She hadn't lost him that day, though, so she hadn't lost him those times, either. He'd made certain she'd stayed safe. But that had been easy since there hadn't been any more attempts on her life.

Hell, she didn't even think the cut brake line had been an attempt on her life but on her mother's, as a warning to Wendy to destroy the evidence.

Maybe it had been. But the thing was, Luther didn't make empty threats. If he was after her parents, wouldn't he have tried again?

But nothing had happened at their house, either.

Maybe Luther had just had all his energy and his crew focused on taking out the eyewitness then. But Rosie Mendez hadn't been as easy to kill, as he must have counted on her being. Of course, she had the Payne Protection Agency and Clint Quarters guarding her.

"Aren't you taking this thing a little far?" Dubridge asked from his desk.

Hart glanced over at the dark-haired detective. "What thing?"

Spencer lowered his voice so the other detectives in the bull pen wouldn't overhear. "Acting like her boyfriend…"

Hart gestured at Keeli, who was sprawled in the chair next to Spencer's desk. "You have a girlfriend," he said. "Maybe we'll have to double-date sometime."

Both Keeli and Spencer glared at him.

He grinned. "Just kidding."

"You do seem pretty convincing," Keeli remarked.

Just because he didn't hate the person he was protecting, like she did, didn't mean that Hart had feelings for Wendy. He just wanted to keep her safe—especially now—because he knew what the news Parker had given him meant.

He shrugged. "It's not like Luther hasn't figured out yet that the chief hired Payne Protection." He glanced around the detective bull pen. And it was pretty damn obvious that everybody in the police department had figured it out, too.

He didn't care about his cover being blown, though. He only cared about keeping Wendy safe.

Since Luther hadn't been able to get rid of the eyewitness, he definitely had to destroy the evidence. And Wendy stood between him and that evidence.

Mills wasn't just going to threaten her now. He had to make good on those threats. He would, undoubtedly, focus all of his time and energy, and whatever members of his crew had survived the attempts on Rosie Mendez's life, to take out Wendy.

Fear curled low in Hart's gut, making him feel sick with worry for her. She had to stop fighting his protection. She needed him.

But why did he feel as if he needed her?

Probably just because, for so many years, he'd tried to take down Luther Mills and it was finally now possible—but only with Wendy's evidence. The eyewitness wasn't as credible a source as DNA and fingerprints and ballistics reports. While Luther's high-powered attorney could discredit the witness, there was no discrediting Wendy. She was too good. She knew what she was doing when it came to evidence.

When it came to protecting herself, she was too trusting. She thought she could rely on her fellow officers. But that wasn't the case. And if the chief had told her who had tried to kill the witness, she had to know that she couldn't trust anyone but him.

Yet when she stepped out of the chief's office, she looked anywhere but at Hart—as if trying to pretend she hadn't even seen him. But he'd caught those furtive glances she'd been sending his way through the chief's office window. She was well aware that he was there.

So her acting like she wasn't aware irritated him— especially since she'd just tried ditching him when she'd slipped out of the lab while he was on the phone. To irritate her, he called out, "There's my girl!"

Detectives glanced up from their desks and watched as Hart headed straight for her. He tugged her up against him and planted a kiss on her lips.

He hadn't kissed her since that morning in her driveway. For the past week, he'd been careful to stay out of her parents' sight. He'd even lain as low as he possibly could around the police department. But officers must have noticed his presence because there had not been another threat or attempt on her life.

That was before Clint had whisked the eyewitness away to an undisclosed location. Nobody would find her. So Luther Mills was bound to turn all his attention to Wendy.

And so would Hart.

While she stood frozen in his embrace, he moved his mouth across hers, deepening the kiss. Something happened every time his lips touched hers. Something jolted him into feeling desire again. Lust…

He'd thought he was beyond all that—after what he'd been through. He knew now that he'd never loved Felicity's mother. Hell, he hadn't even known Monica—until it was too late. By the time he'd learned how selfish and unfaithful she was, she was pregnant. He'd tried to make it work. But he'd been the only one trying.

Lust had brought him so much pain that he'd vowed never to succumb to it again. But he felt it now, coursing through his body, heating his skin, making his pulse pound. He would have gone on kissing Wendy if not for the catcalls that reminded him they were not alone.

Reluctantly he lifted his head from hers. Then he flashed a grin at the room.

"So that's why you've been hanging around the department," an older detective remarked. "I thought you were either here on a bodyguard assignment or you were trolling to get your job back with RCPD."

Hart shook his head.

"So things are good at the Payne Protection Agency?" the detective asked.

Hart shrugged. "I'm happy, but that's more for personal reasons than professional reasons." He slung his arm around Wendy's shoulders and pulled her close to his side. Her body was tense and stiff against his. He leaned down and advised her, "Smile."

Her lips curved, but when she looked up at him there was no love or amusement in her green eyes. Instead, anger glimmered.

"You shouldn't have done that," Wendy whispered between gritted teeth.

He probably shouldn't have—because his pulse kept

racing and his body kept throbbing with desire for her. Since he was pretty damn sure everybody was aware that he was her bodyguard, he hadn't needed to kiss her to perpetuate the boyfriend act. Something had driven him to do it.

Or someone…

He glanced over at Dubridge. Instead of looking jealous, which for some reason Hart had perversely wanted to make him, Spencer was grinning broadly.

Had he goaded Hart into overplaying his hand? Why? For his own amusement? It wasn't like he was playing matchmaker or anything. Hart doubted there was a romantic bone in Spencer Dubridge's big body.

Keeli was studying the detective through narrowed blue eyes, as if trying to surmise his motivation, as well. She looked away quickly, though, and shook her head, as if she'd already given up trying to figure him out.

"Congrats, Wendy," a female detective called out. "You finally got your man."

Wendy's face flushed bright red. But she held on to her smile as they walked out of the room. The minute they were outside the door to the detectives' bull pen, though, she pulled away and whirled toward him.

Hart realized the increased danger wasn't just from Luther Mills but from Wendy herself. She looked mad enough to kill *him*.

Just when Wendy thought she couldn't be any more humiliated…

Hart had to make a scene like he had in the middle of the bull pen. And, of course, he'd chosen to do it when just about every single desk in the big area had had someone at it.

The minute they stepped into the hall, she pulled away from him. Her jaw ached, she'd been clenching her teeth so tightly. She told him now what she'd wanted to tell him then. "Don't touch me!"

He stepped back and held up his hands, as if silently promising he wouldn't. But he continued to hover too close to her when she returned to the lab to retrieve her purse and car keys.

"You are not going to need those," he said as he pointed to the key ring.

The keys were for her car. She'd only borrowed her mother's that one day—while hers had, ironically, been getting new brakes and tires.

"I am not leaving my car in the parking garage," she informed him.

He nodded. "You sure as hell are. We're not taking any chances anymore."

"We haven't," she said. "Nothing else has happened this past week."

"Not to you," he agreed. "But it sure as hell happened to Rosie Mendez."

She sucked in a breath as she thought of the trauma the young woman had endured. Wendy had met Rosie at the scene of her younger brother's murder. She'd collected evidence from the scene and from Rosie herself, who'd been covered in her brother's blood. Since she was an only child, Wendy hadn't been able to imagine the depth of Rosie's pain over the loss of her sibling. But she had felt horrible for her.

"The chief told me that she's safe now," Wendy said. She desperately hoped that was true.

Hart shrugged. "Nobody knows where she and Clint went, so it'll be hard for anyone to find them."

"Good."

"But that means you're in even more danger than you already were," he warned her. "Luther will focus all his attention on getting rid of you now."

"The chief told me that, too," she said, shaking her head in silent protest of what else he'd said. Nobody she worked with could also be working for Luther Mills. It just wasn't possible.

"You don't believe him?" Hart asked. "Or you don't want to believe him?"

"I want to go home," she said.

She wanted to make sure her parents were safe. Luther wanted her to get rid of the evidence and she was afraid he might try to harm her parents to coerce her to do that.

"I'll take you home," Hart said.

She didn't argue with him, just followed him down the corridor to the elevator, which they took up to the lobby. The minute the doors slid open, he put his arm around her again. She tensed and tried to pull away.

"I told you not to touch me…"

He leaned closer and whispered, "I don't trust you to not try to ditch me again."

She was so angry over the scene he'd made that she might have if he hadn't been holding on to her. She tried to veer toward the rear exit of the lobby, which would bring her to the employee parking garage, but Hart steered her toward the front doors instead.

She probably looked as panicked as she felt at the thought of being alone with Hart again because one of the guards manning the screening machines at the entrance glanced up at her. She could have called the officer over, could have told her that Hart was hassling her, but it would have been stupid to make a scene that would get back to the chief. He already thought she was an idiot.

She'd seen it on his face as he'd lectured her about the dangers of being too trusting. Her parents had raised her to always look for the good in people, though. And despite all the years she'd seen the bad at crime scenes, their lesson had stuck.

Maybe too well…

As she and Hart walked past the security officer, the young woman smiled, almost enviously, at them.

"Have a good evening" was all Wendy told her.

The woman winked. "Thanks, but I don't think it'll be as good as yours."

For years Wendy had wished Hart Fisher had acted like he was acting now with her: like he was attracted to her. But she knew this was only an act, just part of his job as her bodyguard.

A job he had already admitted he hadn't wanted.

She knew protecting her was the only reason he kept her as close as he did. When they stepped outside, he positioned her body between his and the building, so that she was shielded from any threat. But he'd parked in the open lot across the street from the police department, so they would eventually have to cross traffic to reach his Payne Protection SUV.

The light seemed to be stuck on the Do Not Walk symbol. As more pedestrians joined them, Hart drew her closer to him. Her body tingled everywhere his touched hers. And, despite the cool autumn breeze blowing leaves around the sidewalk and across the street, heat rushed through Wendy. She focused on that damn red light because she didn't want to look at him. But she could feel him staring at her.

His gaze drew hers like there was a connection between them, a connection that had her standing taller, raising her head…as he began to lower his. Her gaze slipped from his warm brown eyes to his lips. They were so chiseled, like every feature on his handsome face.

How could she not have a crush on him? It was unfair that he looked like that.

That was the remark she had casually made to a coworker years ago. That it was unfair he was so handsome.

From that remark, the rumor of her crush must have spread throughout the rest of the station. Remembering that they were still within sight of the building had her drawing back—quickly—before he kissed her again.

He jerked away from her, as well, and straightened, as if he'd just remembered where they were.

Maybe he wasn't just acting attracted to her.

Maybe he was?

No. She was being ridiculous. He'd probably just noticed someone standing near them that he'd wanted to fool. But he was starting to fool her, too. At least, she felt like a fool.

She looked around to see if anyone had witnessed their near kiss and noticed that everyone else had already started across the street. The walk signal had finally lit up.

A ragged sigh shuddered out of Hart. "It's about time," he murmured. Then he cupped her elbow in his palm and started leading her across the street. But they never made it to the parking lot.

Not before they heard the crunch of metal as a vehicle slammed into the ones already stopped at the red light, as if to shove them aside. And it must have moved them because suddenly there was nothing stopping the big white van barreling straight for them.

Luther Mills studied his lawyer across the metal table in the small room where Luther was allowed to confer privately with his visiting counsel. He usually used these meetings for things other than conferring. He gave the lawyer messages or other things to deliver for him. And he used the lawyer's phone to make calls he didn't want to risk anyone overhearing—the way someone must have overheard and reported his earlier calls.

How the hell else had Lynch known there was a leak? And the chief had to have known or he wouldn't have hired Payne Protection to guard everyone associated with this damn trial. Somehow Lynch knew Luther intended to take them all out.

The former Bureau chief was making that damn hard for him, though.

So today the lawyer had wanted to talk strategy. The guy was slick, from his greased-back hair to the toes of his shiny shoes. He was the best that money could buy, or so Luther had been told.

Now he was beginning to wonder.

"I think you should accept a plea," the guy recommended. "Manslaughter, involuntary homicide."

"Is that hot little assistant DA offering pleas?" Luther asked.

"To the shooters apprehended during the attempts on the eyewitness's life," the lawyer said.

Luther cursed and shook his head. He had already made damn sure that nobody accepted a plea deal from Jocelyn Gerber. If they did, they knew they would wind up deader than Javier Mendez.

At least he hadn't made Javi suffer…*much*.

"They won't," Luther confidently assured him. "And even if she offered me a plea, I'd tell her what she could do with it…"

The lawyer sighed. "Miss Mendez wasn't the problem," he said. "I told you that eyewitness testimony can be easily discredited."

The guy had obviously never met Rosie Mendez. Luther hoped that he never would, either. *She* would not be easily discredited. She was too strong and too damn stubborn. If she wasn't, she would have already wound up dead, like her brother.

"It's the DNA and the fingerprints that will put you away for life," the lawyer warned him. "Juries eat that up."

"They can't eat what they aren't fed," Luther said.

"That evidence won't make it to trial." And neither would the woman who'd collected it. If she wasn't already, Wendy Thompson would be dead soon.

Chapter 7

"I'm sorry," the sitter said as Felicity scampered into the nursery off Sharon's office. "I didn't know where else to go when I couldn't reach Mr. Fisher. And I'd picked her up here that night a week ago…"

"It's fine," Parker assured the older woman. She was probably close to his mother's age, but she didn't have Penny Payne-Lynch's vivaciousness. Her hair was mussed, as if she'd just woken from a nap, but with the dark circles beneath her eyes, she didn't look rested. She looked exhausted.

"I just really feel that I should check on my mother," the woman said. "She's older now…"

Parker narrowed his eyes and studied the woman's tense face. She wouldn't meet his gaze. She was obviously lying, and she was so uncomfortable about it that his silent scrutiny unsettled her.

She blurted, "She's just been so difficult lately."

He arched a brow. "Your mother?"

Her face flushed. "Felicity. I...I lied about my mother."

He couldn't believe how easily he'd got the confession from her. Maybe he should have become a detective like his brother Logan had been during their years with the River City Police Department. But Parker had enjoyed Vice—back then he'd had quite a few of his own.

Now he was a happily married man with kids of his own. Maybe that was how he'd developed this new, silent interrogation skill. It was the one his mother had always had; an ability to see whenever one of her children was lying to her.

Of course, his mother sensed things nobody else could well before they happened. Parker didn't want that ability himself, but lately he'd begun to have those kinds of feelings—like bad things were going to happen. He'd had them about Clint Quarters and Rosie Mendez.

But they were safe now, and that bad feeling hadn't eased any. In fact, it had seemed to intensify, tying his stomach into knots. Maybe those bad things were going to happen to someone else.

Like Hart Fisher and Wendy Thompson.

"Felicity has been whining that she wants to see her father," the woman said, her brow furrowed, "and someone she keeps calling Winnie."

Winnie?

"Wendy?"

"Winnie!" the little girl said as she appeared in the doorway to the nursery. "Is Winnie here?" She must have seen his confusion because she held up her doll. "Winnie. She looks like my dolly. But my dolly's name is Annie."

To the little girl, Wendy must have been "Winnie." Parker nodded and smiled with the realization that she could not say "Wendy" correctly and that she thought the evidence technician looked like a rag doll.

She wrapped her little arms around the doll and hugged her tightly. "I want to see Winnie!"

"Winnie's not here, honey," Parker said, using his best Soothing Daddy voice.

But he must have only reminded the little girl of her father because she burst into tears. "I want my daddy!" she choked out between sobs and hiccups.

"See," the babysitter murmured as she edged toward the door. "This is what I've been dealing with for days."

"I'm sorry," Parker said, and he felt responsible.

He was the one who'd assigned Hart the difficult job of protecting the evidence tech. Hart had left the police department because, as a single father, he hadn't been able to work the long hours of a detective any longer.

And Parker had assigned him long hours. He'd made sure, though, that another bodyguard, on loan from his brothers' agencies, had given Hart some time every day to see his daughter.

But of course, he needed to sleep during that time,

too, so he probably hadn't been spending as much time with her as either of them would like.

"I'll find your daddy," he assured the little girl. He reached for her but she stumbled back, as if afraid of him. He looked to her babysitter for help, but the woman must have assumed he had it handled because she was gone. She'd left his office when he'd had his attention on the child.

He felt a flash of annoyance. Hart needed a new sitter. Nobody Parker knew would abandon a child in distress. But then, he'd been raised by the best and had the best co-parent in his amazing wife.

"I'll call your daddy," Parker assured the little girl. Hart's contact number was already on the screen of his cell phone since he'd just tried it a little while ago. He pressed it again, but the call went immediately to voice mail.

Why the hell wasn't Hart answering?

That damn sixth sense of his mother's began to overcome Parker in that he just *knew* something had happened. Something *bad*.

Her body was stiff and unmoving beneath his. Hart couldn't even feel her breathe. But before rolling off her, he looked around for the van that had nearly struck them. Various other vehicles had pulled to the sides of the street, some bearing dents and creases from the van.

But he didn't see the vehicle itself. It was gone.

"Are you okay?" Hart asked as he stared down into Wendy's ashen face.

Her beautiful green eyes were open but glazed, as if

she was in shock. Like she had probably been the day the car had crashed into the tree. But at least that day, she hadn't been hurt. He wasn't so sure about now.

"Are you okay?" he asked again as he brushed his fingers across her cheek.

She shivered at his touch then finally nodded.

"Are you sure?" he asked with concern. When he'd put his body between hers and the van, he'd knocked her to the asphalt. Hard.

"Yes." She gasped for air. "I just lost my breath for a moment."

He cringed with regret. "I knocked the wind out of you. I'm sorry." He wrapped his hands around her waist and lifted her carefully to her feet.

"You saved my life," she said, and her eyes widened with concern. She looked him up and down as she grasped his arms. "Are you all right? Did you get hit?"

"No." But just as he said it, a vehicle whizzed past them, honking as it nearly struck him. Hart grabbed her arm to escort her onto the sidewalk next to the lot where he'd parked the Payne Protection SUV. She grimaced and he noticed that the sleeve of her jacket was torn.

He had knocked her down too hard. He quickly loosened his grasp and inspected the damage. It looked as though the jacket had taken the worst of it; the material was torn but not saturated with blood. Her skin still could have been scraped, though, or, at the very least, she would be bruised. "You are hurt."

She shrugged. "It's nothing compared to the damage that van would have done if you hadn't pushed me out of the way. Thank you."

He knew that hadn't been easy for her to say—not with how angry she'd been with him just moments ago for kissing her in the middle of the bull pen in the River City Police Department.

Had the driver of the van been waiting all day for them to leave? He doubted it. It made more sense that someone within the department had seen him waiting for her outside the chief's office. When they'd headed to the lab to get her stuff, he'd headed outside to get the van and run them down.

"We need to get out of here," he said.

He—they—couldn't trust anyone...but Payne Protection. He clicked the fob for the SUV and pulled open the passenger's door. Careful of her injured arm, he helped her onto the seat and shut the door before rushing around the front to the driver's side.

As he slid behind the wheel, his cell phone began to vibrate inside his pocket. He'd felt it earlier, but he'd been focused on the van and keeping Wendy alive. Now he pulled it out and glanced at the screen. "Parker."

"Aren't you going to answer it?" Wendy asked.

He shook his head. "No."

"But he's your boss," she said. "Don't you have to?"

"We're just a few minutes away from the agency," Hart said. He rolled down the driver's window and swiped his card through the meter at the gate, which slowly rose. So slowly that he nearly drove through it in his haste to get out of the lot. He needed to get her away from the police department before that van circled around and tried for them again.

She reached across the console and grasped his arm. "But we need to file a report—"

"That's why we're going to the agency," Hart said. "We need to talk to Parker." His phone vibrated again, and he saw that his boss had left him a voice mail. He pressed harder on the accelerator, speeding down the street.

"Parker doesn't take reports," she said. "He isn't a police officer any longer."

"Exactly," Hart said. "That's why we can trust him."

Wendy sighed. "I know there was one bad officer." The chief had brought her up to speed during their meeting.

"And even Lynch doesn't think that one rookie was the only officer helping Luther Mills," Hart said. Parker had shared that information with him, so that he would stay alert to danger.

He hadn't stayed alert enough. He'd allowed her to distract him. In the lobby and on the sidewalk...

If he hadn't been so focused on her, on thinking about kissing her again, maybe he would have noticed the van sooner. Maybe he could have got a look at the driver, so he could identify him. Or a glimpse of the plate so he had at least a few of the numbers.

That was another reason he hadn't wanted to stay to file a report. He had nothing to report, but that he'd nearly let Wendy get killed again.

She said nothing now, just stared out the window as he drove. Her face was so pale that her freckles stood out in stark contrast on the bridge of her cute nose and the curves of her cheekbones.

He arrived at Payne Protection within a couple of minutes, which probably wouldn't have even given him enough time to play Parker's voice mail had he been so inclined. But with Wendy in the vehicle, he hadn't been inclined. He'd needed to be focused on the road instead and on the rearview mirror, making certain nobody followed them.

Nobody had.

He breathed a sigh of relief as he pulled into the parking lot of the agency. Here was backup; here was safety. But the minute he and Wendy stepped inside the office, she was attacked.

She staggered back on her feet, nearly falling over, but Hart caught her shoulders. Holding her steady, he glanced down at the small body that had nearly knocked her over.

Felicity had hurtled herself at Wendy.

Or Winnie…as she'd called out. Her arms wrapped around Wendy's waist, she buried her tearstained face in Wendy's flat stomach.

Hart felt that weird twinge in his chest now. Maybe it was just jealousy. Since his mother's death, he had been the only one Felicity had wanted for comfort when she was upset.

"What's wrong, sweetheart?" he asked as he dropped to his knees next to his daughter. And why had she sought comfort from the woman who was nearly a stranger rather than him?

But then, he hadn't been very available to his daughter this past week—not with the hours he'd been keeping as Wendy's bodyguard. Even when another Payne bodyguard had taken over so he could sleep, he'd been sleeping instead of spending quality time with his little girl.

Wendy had spent no time at all with her. How had the little girl got so attached from their one meeting a week ago?

Wendy gently patted Felicity's head, smoothing her hand over the pale blond hair. "It's okay, honey," she said. "Don't cry…"

But Felicity's little body shook with her sobs. And Hart's heart broke with her pain.

"Sweetheart," he said, "what's wrong?" He glanced up at his boss, who stood in the doorway behind the little girl, when he asked that question.

"Her sitter brought her here," Parker said, "after she couldn't get hold of you. Then I tried—"

"I had a good reason for missing your calls," he said. "But yours were the only ones I missed."

Parker nodded in acceptance of his word. "I think you need a new sitter."

"I want Winnie," Felicity murmured.

"Wendy isn't a babysitter," Hart told her.

She was an evidence tech—one in extreme danger, which put anyone around her in extreme danger, as well. She really shouldn't be around his little girl. But he wasn't sure he would have been able to pry Felicity off her at the moment. And he wasn't really sure that he wanted to. Once he'd pushed aside his flash of jealousy, he was pleased that she'd finally connected with another female.

"I want Winnie…" his little girl murmured.

So did Hart—after all the times he'd kissed her. But

more than he desired her, he wanted to keep her safe—and his daughter happy.

Was there a way that he could manage both?

"This is a bad idea," Wendy whispered. She'd leaned across the console so her lips were close to Hart's ear.

He shivered, as if a chill had passed over him. Instead of paling, his skin flushed. He glanced at her and agreed. "Probably..."

"Then why...?"

"Because I need to protect you."

Need. Now she shivered at the tone of his deep voice and the look in his brown eyes when he glanced at her. They seemed an even warmer brown than usual, like heated milk chocolate. But being her bodyguard was just his job, protecting her just his latest assignment.

She needed to remind herself of that; that their being together was just an act. It wasn't real.

"Winnie, we going to your house?" a little voice, shaking with excitement, asked.

Wendy looked into the back of the SUV, where Hart had buckled his daughter into a booster car seat. Felicity's tears had dried, but her eyes were still puffy, her cheeks still flushed.

"Yes," she answered the little girl. She glanced at Hart again and murmured through clenched teeth, "I still think it's a bad idea."

"Your parents' house is very secure," Hart said as if trying to convince himself.

That wasn't what she was worried about, though. She was worried about confusing the little girl and fooling her parents, and maybe herself, as well, into thinking this act was real.

"Cooper's team is already in place protecting the house and your mom and dad," Hart continued, lowering his voice to a low whisper. Not that Felicity was listening; she was singing to herself about going to Winnie's house. "With the exception of his sister Nikki, Cooper's team is comprised entirely of ex-Marines. They're very good at protection."

And so was he.

If he wasn't, she would have already died in a crash. Either the one where the brakes on her mother's car had been cut or when the van had tried to run them down.

She knew neither incident was an accident. Luther Mills was coming after her. So it wasn't safe for anyone to be around her—her parents or Hart's little girl.

Wendy didn't want any of them getting hurt because of her. Not even Hart…despite how much he infuriated her. But that kiss hadn't just infuriated and embarrassed her.

It had also excited her. Even now her body hummed with it, her pulse racing and her heart pounding. She wanted him to kiss her again. She needed him to kiss her again, and not just for the act.

For real…

He didn't even seem aware of her right now, though. He kept glancing into the rearview mirror. She figured he was checking on his daughter.

It must have hurt him to see her as upset as she'd been at the agency office. It had hurt Wendy.

The little girl's tears and emotional distress shouldn't

have affected Wendy as much as they had. In the course of her job, she saw people all the time who were in pain and emotional distress.

Like Rosie Mendez had been after witnessing her brother's murder…

No one had died in front of Felicity Fisher. She had just been upset because she'd been missing her daddy and *Winnie*. How had she got so attached to Wendy so quickly? Why had she sought her out for comfort instead of her father?

But Wendy felt it, too, the pull between them; she and the little girl had made some connection that first night, as if they recognized each other as kindred souls, which was silly. They had nothing in common.

Wendy had always been a tomboy while Felicity Fisher was a little princess, as beautiful as her mother probably was.

She smiled at the child who sweetly smiled back at her. Then she glanced beyond her, through the rear window, and realized what Hart had really been looking at…

The white van that was following the SUV. "Is that the same one…from the street?" she asked. The one that would have run them over had Hart not reacted as quickly as he had.

"It's not backup," her bodyguard replied, a muscle twitching in his cheek, above his tightly clenched jaw.

That night he'd taken her to the Payne Protection Agency with the chief, she'd noticed that every vehicle in the lot had been a black SUV, like the one they were driving.

No. The white van did not belong to a Payne Protection bodyguard. The front bumper and passenger-side fender were crumpled, like the van had struck a tree. Or other cars.

She sucked in a breath. "That is the van." She had no doubt that the person who'd tried running her down was now following them.

"Did they follow us to the agency?" she asked.

Hart shook his head. "No. I checked. I swear, I checked to make sure nobody was following us."

It didn't matter. Despite Hart's efforts, the driver of the van had found them. He must have recognized Hart as a Payne Protection bodyguard and realized where he was going. And now he must have realized he'd been noticed because the van sped up, bearing down on the SUV just as it had borne down on them in the street.

Hart had saved her then.

Could he save her and his daughter now?

Chapter 8

How the hell had he missed it?

The van must have followed him from the police department to the Payne Protection Agency. But Hart had carefully watched the rearview mirror during that drive. That was why he hadn't played Parker's message and why he had tried to ignore Wendy's distracting presence.

He'd been mostly successful with that—successful enough that he should have noticed the damaged van behind them before now.

The driver must have carefully hung back just far enough that Hart would miss seeing the tail.

He silently cursed himself and his carelessness. Unless…the driver had realized he was a Payne Protection bodyguard and that he would head back to the agency. Maybe Luther even had some crew members watching the agency office building. The drug king-pin was smart; that was why he'd eluded prosecution for so long.

The van wasn't hanging back anymore. It was speeding up, speeding toward the SUV just as it had sped toward Wendy on the street. He had to protect her now like he had then.

But she wasn't the only one about whom he was worried. He'd buckled Felicity's booster-style carrier tightly into the seat, so that the straps safely crossed her little body without risking harm to her neck or back.

But still…if they were hit hard enough from behind, she could be hurt. She was so small, so delicately boned.

He pressed harder on the accelerator, trying to gain some distance from the van. But it kept coming—faster and faster.

"Lose it," Wendy hissed at him through lips curved into an obvious fake smile for Felicity's sake.

Tension and fear gripped Hart. "It's going to get dangerous."

Wendy nodded with understanding. She focused her attention on his daughter. "We're going to play a game with Daddy," she told the little girl.

"What game?" Felicity asked.

"Roller coaster," Wendy said gleefully.

"Roller coaster?" the little girl repeated, sounding more frightened than gleeful.

That was what scared Hart—scaring his daughter. But he had no choice. He had to lose that van for her protection. The driver was bearing down on them too fast.

"Don't you like roller coasters?" Wendy asked.

Felicity shook her little blond head. "No, I'm too little to ride them."

"You're just the right size for this ride," Wendy said. "It's going to be fun!"

Just as the van was about to slam into the rear bumper of the SUV, Hart jerked the steering wheel, making a sharp right turn onto another street.

Wendy squealed with feigned delight. "See?" she exclaimed to the little girl. "Isn't it fun?"

A glance in his rearview mirror confirmed two things. One, that his daughter wasn't as excited about this ride as Wendy was pretending to be. And two, that he hadn't lost the van. The driver, whom he couldn't see through the van's tinted windshield, made the sharp turn behind him and sped up.

Hart yanked the wheel again, this time to the left, and he did it so sharply that the SUV careened around the corner on two wheels.

Wendy squealed again and started laughing.

Little giggles finally echoed her laughter and Felicity called out, "Do it again, Daddy! Do it again!"

He had no choice. The van was not easy to shake. If the guy had followed him, it was no wonder that Hart hadn't made the tail on the way to Payne Protection. But as good as the driver was, Hart was better.

Or maybe, with his daughter and Wendy in the vehicle with him, he just had more motivation to be successful. He had to keep them safe. His daughter, because she was his life. And Wendy...

She was beginning to mean so much more to him

than an assignment. Despite the risk of whiplash if they were struck, she stayed turned in her seat, facing his daughter. Smiling at her, laughing with her...

God, he wanted to kiss her again. Deeply. Passionately.

He wanted her so badly, more than he could ever remember wanting any other woman. His ex-wife had been beautiful, but Monica's beauty had only been on the surface. It wasn't like Wendy's beauty, which went so deep that it distracted the hell out of him.

He focused again on the rearview mirror, catching a glimpse of his smiling daughter before he saw the van.

He hadn't lost it yet.

But he would.

He would do anything to protect his daughter and Wendy.

He careened around another corner as the two females squealed with delight. Wendy was brilliant to have invented this *game* for his daughter, so Felicity wouldn't be scared.

But it was clear that Wendy was scared as one of her hands gripped the console and the other gripped the back of her seat. She kept the smile on her beautiful face for Felicity's sake, but that smile never quite reached her eyes.

He had turned onto a long, straight stretch of road with no curves to turn to escape that van. All he could do was press hard on the accelerator and hope to outrun it.

But it kept gaining on them.

Just before its crumpled front bumper collided with

their rear one, Wendy announced, "Now we're playing bumper cars."

The van struck them, propelling the SUV forward.

All Hart could do was tightly grip the wheel and hope that he didn't lose control.

"Do you think this is really a good idea?" Wendy asked as fear rushed over her again. Her face hurt from the smile she'd forced herself to wear for Felicity, but all the while her heart had pounded so hard and so fast.

"I lost the tail," Hart assured her.

She shook her head. She wasn't talking about the tail, although she was surprised he had managed to shake it, especially after the van had collided with their rear bumper. The SUV must have been reinforced, though, and the van had done more damage to itself than to it.

When Hart had accelerated again, he'd managed to outrun it. Or so she hoped. She hadn't noticed it following them from the parking lot across from the police department to the agency, either. But maybe the driver had known where they were headed then.

Did he know now? She glanced anxiously around her parents' driveway and the street.

Could the van be out there? Could the driver be waiting for them to step out of the SUV to try to run them down again?

Hart had already got out and, with Felicity cradled in one arm, had come around and opened the passenger door for Wendy. No van gunned its engine and steered toward them. But then, the driver of the van wasn't after Hart and his daughter.

He was after *her*.

If she stepped out, it could appear. She glanced toward the street, to where a Payne Protection SUV partially blocked the driveway. With all the trees in the front yard, there was no way the van could get to them. But that wasn't why Wendy hesitated before stepping out of the SUV.

She hated lying to her parents. She didn't want them or Felicity to think that she and Hart were any more than assignment and bodyguard. If she told them the truth, they would be so scared. She'd convinced the child that the van smashing into them was just a game. But if Felicity had realized what was really going on, she would have been terrified.

Wendy shivered as she stepped out onto the driveway. It had nothing to do with the cool breeze whipping bright-colored leaves around the yard and across the driveway. It was a different kind of chill that gripped Wendy—the cold chill of dread.

"You're cold," Hart said. "We should get in the house."

Wendy shook her head and murmured again, "This is a bad idea."

"It's fine," he said, as if dismissing her concerns. From the tension in his jaw and his big muscular body, she could tell that he was worried, too.

He knew.

No. It wasn't fine. She was already becoming too attached to his daughter. And if her parents met the little girl…

It was too late, though.

The front door to the house opened and her mother

limped out onto the small porch. "Who do we have here?"

Felicity buried her face in Hart's neck, hiding from Wendy's mom.

"It's okay, sweetheart," Wendy assured the little girl, rubbing her back. "We're at my house. This is my mother."

Despite her still-healing knee, her mother moved quickly down the front steps to join them on the driveway. "Who is this little princess?" she asked, all her attention focused on the child.

While she had retired a few years ago, Margaret Thompson still sounded like the kindergarten teacher she had been for so many years. But the little girl continued to ignore her. So Margaret turned to Hart. "I understand you met my husband…"

Hart's face flushed bright red. But he couldn't have been embarrassed at getting caught in Wendy's bed. It wasn't as if anything had been happening. He hadn't even kissed her yet…that night.

"I'm sorry about that," Hart murmured. "I didn't want to disturb anyone."

She shook her head. Her hair was thick and curly, like Wendy's, but the red had changed to white nearly a decade ago when she'd still been in her late fifties. "It's fine," she said with a smile. "I'm glad you finally came to your senses and realized how amazing my daughter is."

Now heat rushed to Wendy's face and she groaned. "Mom…" Her mother could not have humiliated her more.

"I always knew she was amazing," Hart told her

mother, closing one of his brown eyes in a quick wink, as if he'd shared a deep secret with her.

"And now I know why she's so amazingly beautiful," Hart added. "She looks like you."

Her mother's face flushed and she giggled like a girl, like Wendy and Felicity had been giggling in the SUV. Wendy was surprised that her mother, who'd always been able to tell when *she* was lying, hadn't realized that Hart was.

But then, Wendy had had no idea he could be such a charming liar. He was definitely lying, though. He had never noticed her until he had been assigned to protect her.

Her mother, who was usually not so easily fooled, smiled brightly and clapped her hands together, which drew Felicity's attention. She lifted her head from Hart's shoulder and peeked at Wendy's mom.

"Hey, there, sweetheart," Margaret greeted her. "What's your name?"

The little girl buried her face in Hart's neck again.

"This is my daughter, Felicity," he said by way of introduction.

"I'm sorry I didn't tell you that I was bringing guests home for dinner," Wendy told her mother.

Her mother arched a brow, which had gone as white as her hair, over one of her green eyes. "There's a lot you haven't told me lately."

Wendy felt a twinge of regret. She and her mom had always been so close. But that was why Wendy couldn't tell her the truth. She would be so worried. And she was still recovering from her recent surgery.

"I'm sorry, too, Mrs. Thompson," Hart said. "I hope we're not imposing."

"Not at all," a male voice chimed in. Her father stood on the porch, holding open the front door. "Mags always makes more food than we can eat."

She laughed. "That's your fault," she said, "from all the years you brought home football players for me to feed." She turned back to Hart and his daughter. "I certainly have enough to feed these two."

"I don't know," Hart said. "Felicity might look little but she can really put the food away."

"Put it where, Daddy?" she asked.

He tickled her tummy. "Here."

She giggled and Hart's face...

Wendy's breath caught in her throat as she stared at him. His eyes were so warm, his smile so happy. He loved his daughter so much.

That look chased her chill away as warmth spread through her. She knew now that her crush on him had been silly and superficial, but it hadn't been wrong. He was good-looking and sexy, but more important than that, he was a good man and an incredible father.

Even as that warmth moved through her, Wendy also felt a pang of jealousy that Hart would never look at her like that—with such love. She was only an assignment to him.

"My tummy feels funny," Felicity said.

"It sounds funny, too," Hart said as he tickled her again.

She didn't laugh now. She shook her head. "It feels funny from the roller coaster and the bumper cars."

"Did you all go to an amusement park?" Margaret asked. She wound her arm through her daughter's.

Wendy didn't know if she'd done it so that Wendy could help her walk up the steps of the front porch or so that Wendy couldn't get away from her. Instead of answering the question, though, Wendy suggested, "Let's find some crackers to settle Felicity's stomach."

Margaret leaned on Wendy as they made it up the steps and through the door her father held for them. Wendy avoided meeting his questioning gaze and continued with her mom down the hall toward the kitchen in the back of the house.

Her mother remarked, "You always loved amusement parks, especially the bumper cars. Guess that you still do."

Wendy had had to admit to crashing her mother's car. She just hadn't admitted how it had happened—because she'd had no brakes. If her mother had been driving...

As they stepped into the kitchen, Wendy wrapped her other arm around her mother and hugged her close. She hated the thought that she could have lost her.

Mom pulled back and stared up at her, her eyes narrowed. "What's going on, sweetheart? I know it doesn't take this long for an apartment to get fumigated."

"I told you that this particular strain of cockroaches seems to be resistant to—"

Her mother shook her head. "You're a terrible liar, Wendy."

"I...I'm not—"

"Yes, you are lying," her mother said. "But I think I understand why..."

Wendy tensed. Her mother was very intuitive, but could she have figured out that they were being threatened? That Luther Mills had threatened them?

"You're scared," her mother said.

Oh, God, she had figured it out.

"You're scared of your feelings for Hart," her mother continued. "And for that little girl."

Wendy released a little breath of relief that her mother hadn't figured out the truth.

Margaret Thompson continued. "I saw the way you looked at them, the father and the daughter. That much emotion—that much love—can be frightening."

Wendy shook her head. She didn't love Hart or his little girl. That was ridiculous. She barely knew them. But then Hart, with Felicity still clasped in his arms, followed her father into the kitchen and Wendy felt it. The overwhelming emotion and the fear...

Woodrow Lynch studied the wall of monitors in the security room at the police department. He'd had the footage brought up for the time frame immediately after Wendy Thompson had been in his office.

"What am I looking for?" he asked into the cell phone pressed to his ear.

"Did someone leave either right before or immediately after I left with Wendy?" Hart asked. His voice was pitched low, as if he didn't want his conversation overheard.

Woodrow glanced at the monitors. "It's a busy station," he replied. "People keep coming and going."

"Detectives? Officers? Evidence techs?" Hart asked.

"Yes. Yes. Yes," Woodrow replied.

"We need to investigate them all. See if we can link any of them to Mills." Despite having resigned from being a detective, Hart Fisher hadn't completely left the job.

"Not *we*," Woodrow corrected him. "*I* will do that. You need to keep Wendy safe."

"I'm trying," Hart said, his voice going even lower and deeper with frustration. "But that van, it just kept appearing out of nowhere."

Frustration gripped the chief, as well. "And you think it was a cop driving?"

Woodrow hated that he couldn't trust his own people. But then, the Payne Protection Agency were more his own people than the RCPD…because they were family. Eventually he'd hoped that his officers and support staff would become family, too. He shook his head in self-disgust. And he'd thought Wendy Thompson was naive.

"I just think it was no coincidence that it tried to run us down as we were leaving the building," Hart persisted.

Woodrow didn't believe in coincidences, either. "No. But it doesn't mean a cop was driving the van."

"You're thinking someone could have called the driver," Hart surmised. "That makes more sense about how they were ready for us the minute we stepped out-side. Do you see anyone picking up a phone?"

Woodrow glanced at the monitors again and sighed. "Just about everyone."

A muffled curse emanated from Woodrow's cell. Hart's frustration was turning to anger.

So was his. He was furious that he was no closer to finding the leak in his department than when he'd first learned of Luther Mills's threats.

The rookie cop, who had died while trying to kill Rosie Mendez, hadn't been the only member of the RCPD on Luther's payroll. The young officer hadn't been in the department long enough to know the things Luther had learned about the case, like who had collected the evidence. Some of that could have come from the district attorney's office, so there was obviously a leak there, too.

Woodrow scanned all the faces on those security monitors. Which of them, which one of his officers who had sworn to protect and serve, was selling out justice for Luther Mills?

Woodrow was worried that the rookie cop wasn't going to be the only one who died before Luther's trial. There would be more losses—on both sides of the law.

Chapter 9

"This is like a princess room," Felicity whispered almost reverently as she lay on her back in Wendy's twin bed staring at the soft pink walls and frilly curtains.

"Yes, and finally there is a real princess in this room," Wendy acknowledged.

The little girl glanced nervously around as if she expected to see someone else.

Wendy, sitting on the bed next to her, pressed her fingertip to the tip of Felicity's cute little nose. "You're the princess, sweetheart. You're so pretty."

Felicity reached up and ran her finger over the freckles on Wendy's cheeks. "You're pretty."

Only a child would find her red hair and freckles pretty. Wendy smiled at the little girl's innate sweetness.

"Just like my doll," Felicity said as she tucked the

rag doll beneath the covers and under her arm so it was snug against her side.

Even though dinner had settled the little girl's tummy, she was exhausted, her long, thick lashes fluttering as she struggled to keep her eyes open. So Wendy had brought her upstairs for a nap while Hart and her father did the dinner dishes. That had always been the rule around the Thompson house: her mother cooked and her father cleaned up. And Hart had magnanimously offered to help.

Suck-up.

She couldn't understand why he was laying it on so thick with her parents. Why was he being so ingratiating?

Was that just part of his bodyguard boyfriend cover? Or was he actually that perfect?

She'd always thought so; that was why she'd developed that damn embarrassing crush on him.

"You're the doll, sweetie," Wendy said, and she leaned over and brushed her lips over the little girl's forehead.

Felicity's little rosebud mouth curved into a faint smile. "I'm not a doll, silly…" she murmured as her eyes closed completely.

Wendy moved to stand from where she sat on the edge of the twin bed, but a little hand gripped hers.

"Stay with me," Felicity implored her. "Please, don't leave me…"

A twinge of pain constricted Wendy's heart. Who had left her? Her mother? It was probably why Hart had full custody. Maybe he hadn't fought for it. Maybe his ex had just given it to him, had just given him his daughter.

So Hart was all Felicity had. But he kept leaving her to protect Wendy. She hated that she was causing problems with them. She needed another bodyguard, and Hart needed to focus on his child.

"I'm right here," Wendy assured her. But for how long? Once she got a new bodyguard, she wouldn't see Hart. She wouldn't be in his life or in his daughter's.

"Tell me a story," Felicity pleaded.

Wendy felt a flash of panic. From all her years of working crime scenes, she didn't know any stories fit for a little girl's ears. But she suspected she wouldn't need to say much before Felicity was fast and deeply asleep.

She began. "There once was a princess who—"

Felicity gripped her hand. "No. No princess stories. I don't want to be a princess," she said. "I want to be like you…"

That twinge struck Wendy's heart again but it wasn't of pain; it was of something far more dangerous. "Well, this princess was no regular princess," Wendy assured her. "She was as smart and as strong as she was pretty."

Felicity's lips curved into a smile and she relaxed into the pillow. "That's you…" she murmured.

Now Wendy's eyes stung and she blinked hard. How had this child got to her so quickly? Wendy had never felt any maternal urges to have or even be around kids before. Sure, she oohed and aahed at her friends' new babies and liked all the pictures on their social media pages. But she never offered to babysit.

She'd never thought she would be good with kids. But Felicity wasn't just any kid. She was exceptional.

"This princess is so tough that she isn't afraid of anything," Wendy continued. It was a lie. If this princess was truly her, she was afraid of plenty. Like Luther Mills and his murderous crew.

And Felicity…and the little girl's father.

When Wendy glanced up and saw Hart leaning against the jamb of the open bedroom door, that fear gripped her heart—along with something else.

Something that she was afraid to name.

"This princess…" she murmured as her mind went blank.

"Is fast asleep," Hart finished for her as he stepped through the doorway and approached the bed. He moved around to the other side of the twin bed and sat on the edge. But the mattress was so narrow that he was still close to Wendy.

Too close.

She would have stood to put more distance between them but Felicity's little hand still held hers in a grip that was surprisingly strong. She peered down at the little girl's face, wondering if she was really asleep or just pretending.

Her thick black lashes lay against her smooth cheeks, though. Every feature was perfect, and so different from Hart's that she had to look like her mother. She'd already heard that Hart's ex was a beauty. Now she had no doubt. No wonder everybody had teased her so mercilessly about her crush on him; they'd known how foolish it was. How unrequited it would always be…

But there was something in his gaze as he stared across his sleeping child at her. Something that had heat rushing through Wendy for a reason other than embarrassment.

"You are amazing with her," Hart whispered, and he sounded awed.

"She's amazing," Wendy said. "It's all her."

He smiled with fatherly pride as he gazed down at his daughter. "She is a sweetheart."

Wendy wanted to ask what had happened to her mother, why he had full custody, but she wasn't sure she had the right. She and Hart weren't really dating. He wasn't even her friend. He was just her bodyguard.

"Usually she's so shy with women," he murmured, his brow furrowing slightly as he glanced at Wendy. "But she's taken to you so quickly…"

And she wondered if he considered it too quickly. He would be smart to worry about Felicity becoming too attached since their relationship was only temporary… until Luther Mills was put away for life. But maybe it should end even before then.

It wasn't her business, but she found herself asking anyway. "Why is she shy with women? Isn't she close to her mother?"

He uttered a soft snort and shook his head. "It's hard to be close to someone who's thousands of miles away. My ex remarried and moved to France several months ago. But even before that, Monica didn't have time…" He shook his head. "Or interest."

Wendy gasped. How could a mother not be interested in her own child? Her heart ached for the little girl. "That's her loss," she said, her voice cracking slightly with the emotion overwhelming her. "Felicity is so sweet and special."

"Yes," he agreed, but he was staring at Wendy.

The look in his deep brown eyes had her tingling inside.

Then he murmured, "So are you…"

She glanced back to that open door. Was her father standing there? Why was Hart still putting on the act?

They had no audience.

Felicity was asleep.

"You were so good with her when I was trying to lose that tail," he said. "You turned what could have been a traumatic and frightening experience into a fun adventure for her."

Oh. He was just praising her for how she'd handled his daughter.

She sighed. "That's not an adventure I want to repeat," she admitted. And she realized she had yet to thank him for how he'd saved her life once again. With her free hand, she reached across his daughter and touched his jaw. "You are very good at your job," she commended him. "You have protected me so well…"

But she didn't want him protecting her any longer. For his sake.

And Felicity's.

He had confirmed her suspicion that the little girl had no one else. Hart was all she had.

Before Wendy could say any more, though, he leaned over and brushed his mouth across hers. And she forgot everything but the sensation of his lips moving over hers. Of the heat of his breath and the passion of his kiss…

And that passion rushed over her.

For a moment Hart forgot everything. Where he was. Who he was. He was just a man who wanted a woman—more than he could ever remember that he had wanted anyone before. The desire gripped him, buzzing in his ears, in his body. Tension gripped him, and he groaned.

But then Wendy pulled away and jumped up from the bed. She stumbled back, as if desperate to get away from him. "Why did you do that?" she asked, her eyes wide.

With that buzzing in his ears, in his body, he didn't understand what she was asking. So he just cocked his head in question.

"Nobody's watching us," she said. "Why did you kiss me?"

"Because—"

A giggle interrupted what he'd been about to say—that he'd kissed her because he'd wanted to, because he wanted her. But he looked down at his daughter, who was peeking at them through her lashes.

"Felicity, you're awake," he accused the little imp. He hoped she had just awakened during that kiss and not when they'd been talking about her mother. She was too young to understand that her mother's inability to attach to anyone had nothing to do with her and everything to do with Monica's horrible childhood. Despite all the marriage counseling they'd had, the only thing that made Monica feel better was the attention of men.

Felicity giggled again and opened her eyes. But instead of looking at him, she turned to Wendy. "Daddy kissed you because you're pretty, Winnie," Felicity said. "And because we like you."

Wendy smiled, but the smile didn't entirely reach her bright green eyes. She obviously didn't believe his daughter.

How was she so unaware of how beautiful she was? Of how incredible she was?

He hadn't been lying to her parents or to her. He wasn't acting anymore. He'd kissed her because he couldn't help himself.

And that wasn't good.

She had come to mean too much to him. And he was worried that his attraction to her would distract him from keeping her safe. He needed to call in one of the perimeter guards to protect her.

And she would just have to tell her parents the truth. After spending the evening with Ben and Margaret Thompson, and seeing how much they loved their daughter and how wonderful they'd been with his, he didn't want to lie to them anymore. He also believed that they already suspected something was going on—that Wendy was keeping more than a relationship secret from them.

"Well, sweetheart," he said. "Since you're awake, we can go home now." His daughter would be safer there, with him, while he found her a new sitter. He knew Parker would understand if he had to give up this assignment for Felicity's sake. The Paynes always put family first.

His daughter, however, did *not* understand. "No!" she said adamantly. "I want to stay here. With Winnie."

Wendy smiled as she approached the bed. But her brow was furrowed with concern. "Wouldn't you rather sleep in your own bed? With all your toys?" she asked the child.

Felicity shook her head and burrowed more deeply into the pillow. "I like your bed," she said. Then she held up her doll. "And I got my favorite dolly."

A smile pulled at Hart's lips. His baby had an answer for everything. "Where will Winnie sleep if you're in her bed?" he asked.

"With you," came the little girl's quick reply.

His pulse leaped at the thought. He chuckled. "You're in her bed," he pointed out. "We have no place to sleep."

"I'll make room," she offered with a sleepy smile.

"For both of us?" he teased. "The bed isn't big enough." But it had been big enough for him and Wendy when he'd sneaked through her window a week ago. He glanced at that window now. Could anyone else sneak through there?

That night there had just been a patrol car stationed in the area. There hadn't been the Payne Protection guards that were out there now.

No one would get past them.

Hell, maybe Felicity was safer if they stayed here. If they left now, in the dark, the driver of that white van might think Wendy was with them and try again to drive them off the road.

That wasn't a chance he wanted to take with his daughter, especially if Wendy wasn't there to calm her fears.

But staying here was probably the bigger risk—not to their safety but to his little girl's heart.

She was getting way too attached to *Winnie*. But he was afraid that she was not the only one...

His cell phone vibrated across the surface of the bed-side table. Parker reached out for it quickly, so it wouldn't wake Sharon, who lay with her head on his chest, her arm across his stomach. He grabbed the phone and silenced it, and his hand shook slightly.

He hated getting late-night calls. Nobody ever called at this hour because they had good news. Like someone had shivved Luther Mills in his jail cell and the assignment for the River City PD had ended...

That his team, who were also his friends, was no longer in danger...

Because Parker knew this wouldn't be over; none of the people he'd been hired to protect would be safe until Luther Mills was dead. Or incarcerated for life some-where that he couldn't buy off guards and get orders to his crew on the outside.

Lost in thought, Parker hadn't answered the call fast enough. His cell began to ring again.

Yeah, this was not good news. Good news could be left on voice mail. Not bad news...

"Parker here," he answered.

Just as he'd suspected, it was bad news...

Chapter 10

This is bad.

Fear gripped Hart so tightly that his chest ached.

Very bad.

Hart did not need to hear the concern in his boss's voice to know that. Parker's wasn't the only voice on his cell phone, though. It was a three-way call between him, his boss and one of the perimeter guards, Cole Bentler. He was one of the ex-Marines on loan to Parker from his brother Cooper's team.

Hart had stepped into the hall outside Wendy's bedroom so he could speak freely without his daughter overhearing the conversation. Wendy had stayed in the room with the little girl. He could hear her voice, too, softly emanating through the partially open door as she continued her story of the very brave and independent princess. She didn't realize that she was that princess, not his daughter.

Despite how brave and independent that princess was, she was in danger. Extreme danger...

So they wouldn't hear him, he lowered his voice to ask, "How many did you see?"

"I don't know," Bentler replied. "We just saw movement going through the backyard. It might be nothing. Maybe just some animals..."

Hart was sure it was because anyone who worked for Luther Mills was an animal—just like their boss.

"But that's not what you really think," Parker said, "or you wouldn't have called."

"I know it's smarter to be ready," Cole said, "especially with a child in the house." Hart knew the ex-Marine bodyguard had just recently learned that he was a father himself. He had a little girl, too, so he understood a father's need to protect his children, just like Parker did.

"I shouldn't have brought her here," Hart said in self-recrimination.

"We figured it was the safest place," Parker reminded him. "You have a lot of backup there."

But even Parker knew better than to guarantee Hart's daughter's safety. The Payne Protection Agency was well aware of how much gun power Luther could pull together in a short amount of time.

It was a miracle that Rosie Mendez had not been killed during any of the many attempts on her life. But Clint Quarters was good.

Hart hoped he was that good. He was distracted,

though, with concern for his child and for Wendy Thompson. He had to keep both females and Mr. and Mrs. Thompson safe from harm.

"I've already called in Logan's team to help, too," Parker said.

His brother Cooper's team, all those ex-Marines, was already outside. Surely they would keep anyone from getting inside the house.

Parker must have been worried, really worried, to call in that many guards to help.

"We're right up around the house," Cole assured Hart. "We'll do our best to make sure nobody gets inside." Like Parker, he was careful to offer no guarantees.

In this business, as in the police business, there were no guarantees. A bodyguard, like a lawman, just had to be prepared for every danger.

"Should I come outside to assist?" To stop anyone from getting to the little girl Hart loved and to the people he'd already begun to care about.

"It's better you stay inside," Parker said.

Hart knew why.

Just in case anyone got past those perimeter guards. But if they got inside…would he be able to save everyone?

He reached for his weapon, drawing it from his holster. He would damn well do his best to protect them all.

Wendy gasped as the gun barrel swung toward her. She raised her hands and whispered, "It's okay. It's just me."

Hart lowered the weapon but didn't holster it. He

reached around her and, with his other hand, pulled the bedroom door partially closed. "Is she sleeping?" he asked in a whisper.

She nodded.

If he'd closed the door completely, the little girl wouldn't have heard them talking in normal voices. He obviously wanted to keep an eye on her. And Wendy didn't think it was because he was worried she'd have a nightmare. It was because they were already living in a nightmare.

"What's going on?" she asked, dragging in a deep breath to brace herself. He opened his mouth and, afraid that he might lie to her, she added, "I know something is going on. Who called?"

"Cole Bentler, he's one of the outside guards, and Parker," he said. "Bentler thinks he saw someone or something moving around the backyard."

Wendy tensed then released that breath she'd drawn. "It's probably just my dad." He had a garden that he sometimes tended even after dark.

Hart shook his head. "No. When I came upstairs, your mom and dad were heading to the living room to watch one of their programs."

She tilted her head and listened intently and heard the buzz of the television in the den below them. At least they weren't outside—with whatever or whomever the guard had seen moving around. "Good…"

"I'd prefer that it was your father," Hart said.

"I don't want him getting hurt," she said.

"No bodyguard would have hurt him."

But one of Luther's crew would. She shivered as she realized that they were all in danger. She reached out and pressed her hands against his chest. She wasn't seeking comfort; she was pushing him back. "You need to get out there—to stop them from getting inside the house."

He shook his head. "There are perimeter guards. I need to stay inside to protect you and…" He glanced beyond her through that partially opened door.

His daughter. Felicity was in danger because of her. If only he'd taken the child and left. The farther from Wendy she was, the safer she would be. But it was too late now for her and her father to leave.

"I have a gun," Wendy reminded Hart. "So does my dad. And years ago, when there was that rash of home invasions, Dad converted the basement to a safe room. We can all go down there."

"I thought you didn't want to tell him or your mother about the threats," he said.

She heavily admitted, "I don't want to."

But it seemed as though she had no choice, if they were about to come under attack.

"Bentler wasn't certain that it was people he saw," Hart admitted almost begrudgingly. "He thought it could have been animals moving around the backyard."

Wendy released a ragged sigh of relief. "Animals. That's probably what he saw. My dad's garden attracts all the deer in the area."

Hart didn't look as relieved as she felt, though.

"You could step out the back door and find out for certain," she suggested. "It would only take a minute. Right next to the door is a floodlight that illuminates the whole backyard."

Beneath her palms, she felt the quick pounding in

Hart's chest. She hadn't realized she still touched him, so she pulled her hands away. They tingled from the contact with his hard, warm body.

He offered a slow nod. "I could do that. Just check…"

"And if it's just deer moving around the backyard, then we have no reason to worry."

"Or to tell your parents?"

She nodded now—quickly.

"Wendy, you know they already suspect something's going on," he said. "You should be honest with them."

"Like you're being honest?" she asked.

"I'm keeping your secret," he said.

She should have been grateful for that. Nobody else had deemed to keep her crush secret from him. "Thank you…"

He looked torn, his gaze going from her to the crack in the door behind her.

"I have my gun up here," she assured him.

He tensed more.

"It's in my purse," she said, "which is on a shelf too high for her to reach even if she was awake."

"Get it out," he urged her. "Take the safety off and prepare to shoot anyone who doesn't belong in this house. And if you hear anything—*anything*—out of the ordinary, get Felicity, your parents and yourself to the basement."

She nodded again, quickly and eagerly. "Of course. You're going to go out back?"

"Yes," he said. "I'll turn on that floodlight. And I hope like hell it was real animals Cole saw—deer."

Not animals like the ones that worked for Luther

Mills. She understood. And having seen the crime scenes Luther and his crew left behind, she could not argue with him. They were all animals with no regard for human life.

Now she regretted sending him outside. When he turned to head for the stairs, she grabbed his arm. "Maybe you shouldn't go…"

"Are you scared?"

She nodded again.

"But you're a brave and independent princess," he reminded her with a line from her story.

He must have been as confused as his daughter had been about the fairy tale Wendy had haphazardly spun. She wasn't the princess of whom she'd spoken. His daughter was.

"The story was about Felicity," she said. "But I'm scared for you. Maybe you shouldn't go outside."

"Maybe I won't have to," he said, "once I turn on the floodlight."

She nodded. That was true. That bright bulb lit up the whole backyard. He would be able to see what was out there without going out.

"And Parker called in reinforcements," he said. "It won't just be the ex-Marines out there. His brother Logan's team is on their way, too."

She breathed a little easier. Even Luther Mills wouldn't be bold enough to try something with that many body-guards protecting her and her family.

"Okay, okay," she said. "Just be careful." With one last squeeze of his muscular forearm, she released her hold on him.

He hesitated before heading down the steps. "You be careful, too," Hart urged her and then glanced at that door again.

"I'll protect her," Wendy promised. If it was the last thing she did.

She was sick that the little girl might be in danger because of her. She was the one Luther Mills wanted to threaten, wanted to manipulate into destroying the evidence against him. Despite his threats, she had never been tempted to comply because, if he wasn't stopped, he would just keep hurting more and more people.

Wendy couldn't let that happen. She wouldn't let that happen.

"Protect yourself, too," Hart told her. "And I'll look out for your folks."

She trusted him. She was surprised that he trusted her, as well, with what was clearly most important to him, because he finally turned and descended the stairs to the main level.

Of course, he probably wasn't worried that anyone would get inside, not with all those Payne Protection bodyguards defending the place.

She hoped that he kept his word and just turned on that light. She hoped he didn't step outside the door and put himself in any more danger for her.

He was all his daughter had with her mother thousands of miles away from her. Not that Felicity seemed to miss her. But she couldn't miss what she'd never had. Even her babysitter had abandoned her, like her mother had.

No. Hart was it for Felicity. She couldn't lose her

father. And Wendy, even though she didn't have him, didn't want to lose him, either.

She was tempted to follow him down the stairs, to make sure he did as he'd said and just turned on that light. But she'd made him a promise and she wouldn't break it. She wouldn't risk his daughter's life—not even for his.

She pushed the door open again and headed toward the shelf that held her purse. Even with the gun in her hand, she didn't release the breath she held. It burned in her lungs with the fear that gripped her.

Fear for Hart...

And fear of him, of how the feelings she'd already had for him had intensified. She didn't have some adolescent crush on him anymore. No. What she felt went far deeper than that and scared her almost as much as the thought of whatever Luther Mills might do to her.

Luther stared down at the cell phone in his hand, willing it to ring. The plan was in place now.

The crime scene tech was going to die. He'd given her a chance to destroy that evidence on her own, to walk away from this trial with her life.

But Wendy Thompson had refused to heed his warnings.

So now she was going to pay—with her life—just as the informant had paid for betraying him. And once she was dead, that evidence would be destroyed. He had a plan in place for that, too.

A person he'd already been able to threaten and manipulate, unlike Wendy Thompson.

Maybe she'd felt brave, though, because she had one of those damn Payne Protection bodyguards. Sure, Clint Quarters had protected Rosie. But the stupid ex-vice cop loved the beautiful eyewitness.

Hart Fisher was the one protecting the evidence tech. He was just doing his job. While they might have worked together in the past, they had no present. No future.

Wendy Thompson probably meant more to Luther Mills than she did to Hart Fisher. To Hart, she was just an assignment. To Luther, she was the key to the jail cell, the key that would release him and secure his freedom.

She just had to die for it.

Hart wasn't like Quarters. He wasn't going to risk his life for hers. And he certainly wouldn't give it up.

No. She was going to die tonight.

Luther had no doubt about it. He wouldn't mind if Hart died with her or any other of those damn Payne Protection bodyguards. He'd sent enough gun power to her parents' house to kill them all.

No. There was no way Wendy Thompson was going to survive the night.

Chapter 11

Hart hesitated with his hand on the switch, concerned that if he flipped it, he might compromise the other bodyguards in charge of protecting the perimeter. If some of Luther's crew was out there, Hart could actually end up helping them find and take out the Payne Protection detail.

Or the reverse could be true. He could expose Luther's crew to the guards. Or, he hoped, it was just some hungry deer marauding Ben Thompson's garden.

He drew in a deep breath, tightened his grasp on his weapon and flipped the switch. Wendy had not exaggerated. The floodlight bulb was bright, lighting up the backyard like it was noon instead of nearly midnight. Hart didn't see any deer clandestinely dining on plants.

But there was something out there. He couldn't see people. Just shadows. Hulking shadows...

They probably belonged to the members of Cooper's team. All the ex-Marines were giants: tall, broad, muscular.

Hart should speak with them to find out if they had figured out what Cole Bentler had seen. Their presence alone would have run off the deer and maybe even the other animals—the ones Luther Mills might have sent after Wendy.

Hart unlocked and pushed open the back door. That was when the night exploded with so much gunfire it sounded as if he'd stepped into the middle of a war zone. He ducked down as bullets struck the house, pinging off the aluminum siding. But not every bullet pinged off; some penetrated the siding and the wood beneath it.

"Get down!" he shouted into the house. But he had no idea if Wendy's parents would hear him or if she would. Would she protect his daughter as she'd promised?

Once she'd heard the shots, she would get them all to safety. Wouldn't she? In that basement safe room her father had made?

He needed to get back inside to make sure they did. But maybe it was better that he remain outside to make sure nobody got inside before Wendy got everyone to the basement. Of course, to do that, he had to stay alive.

The shadows took thicker forms as the gunmen advanced. He ducked even lower, hiding behind the shrubbery near the back of the house, and returned fire.

But he was outnumbered. Where the hell was his backup?

Would any of the other guards get around the house in time to help him?

"I'm sorry," he murmured. The apology was for his daughter, for putting himself in a situation where he might not return to her.

He was all she had.

Her mother had gladly given up all of her parental rights to marry another man and move out of the country. And now, with his mother gone, Felicity had no one but him.

And Winnie?

Would Wendy keep his little girl safe?

He had to believe that she would keep the promise she'd made him.

But he wasn't going down without one hell of a fight. Felicity needed him. And he needed Wendy—to protect his daughter and herself.

That was all.

Wasn't it?

Glass shattered, raining down on the floor as Wendy crawled along it, doing her best to shield Felicity. She had one arm around the little girl's trembling body, pulling her along with her.

"Get over here!" Wendy's dad called out from the open door to the basement. "Hurry!"

She barely heard him over the rapid gunfire exploding all around them. She also barely heard the sound of footsteps behind her, but there was a telltale creak of the floorboards. Somebody had got inside the house. She scooped up Felicity and ran for that door. She slammed it shut behind her just as gunfire rang out inside the house, bullets pinging off the steel door.

Years ago, when there'd been home invasions in their neighborhood, her father had turned the basement into a version of a safe room with a steel door and a series of dead bolts on the basement side of that door. Standing on the landing at the top of the stairwell, she and her father both scrambled to turn all those dead bolts and lock out the intruders.

"Come here, sweetheart," her mother called up from the bottom of the stairs. She held out her arms for the scared little girl.

Felicity clung to Wendy, though, her face buried in Wendy's waist. Her shirt grew damp with the child's tears. The sound of gunshots had brutally jerked Felicity awake, and then Wendy had pulled her from her bed to run down the stairs. The first floor had been plunged in darkness but for the glow of the outside light and the flashes of gunfire.

Her father must have turned out the lights so nobody would see them moving around inside. But it had made it difficult for Wendy to move. With all the bullets flying, she'd made certain to stay low, beneath the windows. As they'd crawled across the floor, they'd also crawled over glass.

She picked up the little girl and carried her down the stairs. The fully in-ground basement was brightly lit. Her father's man cave was quite comfortable with its thick carpet, walls finished in stained and painted barn wood, and padded, comfortable furniture.

Wendy carried the little girl to the couch and sat her

on it. "Let me look at you, sweetheart," she said. She had to make sure the child didn't have any glass embedded in her skin, like Wendy could feel in her own palms and knees. But Felicity continued to cling to her. "It's okay, honey. We're safe. We're safe down here."

Up there had been another story entirely. She was surprised she'd managed to get the little girl and herself down to the basement. The gun shoved in the waistband of her dress slacks had proved worthless, as worthless as the one her father grasped in one hand.

She glanced at him and her mother. "Are you both okay?" she asked anxiously. If something had happened to either one of them...

She'd had no time to warn them. No time to prepare them for that sudden burst of gunfire. She hadn't expected it, either. But at least she'd been upstairs. They'd been down where the shooting had started. She looked up and down both of them, checking for blood or wounds. "Are you okay?" she asked again when they had yet to answer.

They nodded, their faces tense and pale with shock. She should have told them what was going on, about the threats. Then maybe they wouldn't have been taken so by surprise. But her father had his gun. Fortunately, he was the type of man who was always prepared to protect his family and himself.

Like Hart...

Where was Hart?

Felicity finally eased away from Wendy and stared up at her. Like Wendy's parents, her face was pale and tense with shock and fear. Her bottom lip quivered as she asked, "Where's Daddy?"

Wendy's heart broke. She didn't know. The shooting must have started the minute he'd turned on that damn light. Why had she suggested it?

Why had she been so naive to think that it was just deer out in the garden? She should have known better. She'd seen the aftermath of what people did to each other. She knew what Luther Mills was capable of.

Was Hart dead?

She couldn't tell his daughter that. Couldn't tell her that her father had risked his life to protect theirs. Not yet…

She didn't want Felicity to know about the danger. She was too young to deal with the gravity of the situation. So she forced her lips to curve into a reassuring smile and told the little girl, "Daddy went outside with his friends."

Hopefully he had met up with the other bodyguards, and they were all protecting each other and not just her and her family.

Whoever had shot at the door must have never reached it. Nobody was trying the handle. And, as she listened intently, she could hear no footsteps overhead.

But shots rang out in the distance. Or maybe it just sounded that way because they were belowground and within concrete walls.

"What are they doing?" Felicity asked, her voice trembling with fear.

Wendy forced her smile wider. "They are doing guy things," she said with a slight shrug as if it was all no big deal. "They must be lighting off fireworks or something…"

Her father grunted his disdain.

But her mother nodded in agreement. "Sounds like fireworks to me."

The little girl leaned back farther and stared up at Wendy speculatively, as if she knew she was lying. Wendy hated that she couldn't be honest with the child. But to tell her the truth would be to scare the innocence out of her. And she couldn't do that.

She lowered her gaze from Felicity's and looked instead at the child's hands and knees. Except for a small scratch on one knee, she appeared unharmed. Just afraid.

The fear gripped Wendy, too. But she kept smiling through it.

"You look like Daddy did when he told me Mommy was gonna get married and move away," she said. "You're acting like you're happy, but I can tell you're not."

A chill chased down Wendy's spine. The little girl was very intuitive. Too intuitive…

So Hart had not been happy about his ex-wife remarrying.

Was it because she'd left her daughter? Or because she'd left him with no chance of ever reconciling?

When he'd told her about it, Wendy hadn't been able to tell how he'd personally felt about his ex. All she'd seen was his love for his daughter.

She listened intently as the gunfire continued outside, flinching at a particularly loud shot.

"Wendy doesn't like loud noises," Margaret Thompson said as she sat next to the child on the couch. "She's not brave like you are."

The little girl glanced up at the older woman then back at Wendy. "Winnie was brave in the car for the roller-coaster ride and the bumper cars."

"That happened in the car?" Ben Thompson asked. "You weren't at an amusement park?"

Wendy shook her head and a thin shard of glass dropped from her hair. "No," she admitted. "There was a van that bumped us."

"Hard," Felicity said. "We bounced around, but Daddy drove fast. He won the game."

"Yes, he did," Wendy said. She hoped like hell he was winning this game, as well.

Wendy's father gestured for her to join him before he walked away from the couch to the other end of his basement man cave, where he had a fully stocked bar and a popcorn machine. But when Wendy moved to follow him, Felicity reached out and clutched at her.

"Don't go, Winnie!" she pleaded, even more intently than she had when Wendy had tried tucking her into bed earlier.

She forced a reassuring smile for the little girl. "I'm just going to make you some popcorn, okay?"

Her father must have heard her because he started up the machine. And her mother quickly fumbled with the TV remote, clicked on the television and flipped through the channels until a cartoon filled the big screen. Hopefully all the noise would drown out the sound of the gunshots ringing out around the basement.

"Wouldn't popcorn be nice with our movie?" Wendy's mom asked the little girl.

All her attention suddenly riveted on the colorful animation on the big screen, Felicity just nodded. Then she let Wendy go as she scooted back on the couch to stare up at the cartoon movie.

Wendy felt a flash of regret that the little girl was no longer holding on to her. For one, she liked comforting her. For another, Wendy didn't want to talk to her father. She didn't want to admit everything that she had been keeping from him and her mother.

Mom joined them, too. She must have sensed her husband's anger because when he opened his mouth, she grasped his forearm and squeezed. "We're okay." She leaned heavily against him, though. Having to run to the basement had probably not been good for her knee. "That's the important thing," she stressed. "That we're all okay."

But she didn't know that. Hart might not be okay. Hart might be dead. The thought horrified Wendy so much that she began to shake. "I have to—"

"Tell us what the hell's going on," her father interrupted, his voice a furious whisper. "Who the hell is this Hart guy that there are multiple gunmen coming after him? What kind of trouble is he in?"

Wendy bit her lip and shook her head as guilt and regret overwhelmed her. "It's not Hart…"

"What?" Her mother gasped in surprise. "That man's not Hart Fisher?"

"No, he's Hart. But the gunmen aren't after him,"

Wendy said. She drew in a deep breath before quietly admitting, "They're after me."

Her mother's grasp tightened on her father's arm again. But this time she used that connection to steady herself as she swayed with shock. "Wendy…"

"Why?" her father asked.

"Luther Mills," she replied.

It was all she needed to say. Her parents lived in River City. They knew about the upcoming murder trial for the notoriously dangerous drug dealer. And while she had never told them that she'd collected the evidence against him, they must have realized it now because her father emitted a ragged sigh and her mother nodded.

"Why didn't you tell us before?" her mother asked.

Wendy sighed. "I didn't want to worry you."

"Why are you here?" her father asked, his eyes narrowed with suspicion. "I never believed your story about the cockroaches."

"Because he didn't threaten just *me*," she said. "He threatened everyone I love. You're everyone I love."

Her mother looked over at the little girl sitting on the couch. Her eyelids had begun to droop again, her lashes shadowing her cheeks.

"We're not *everyone* anymore," Mom said. "Is that why Hart and his daughter came here tonight?"

"Hart Fisher is just my bodyguard," Wendy admitted. "And he had no choice about bringing Felicity. He had to because her babysitter took off."

Her mother gasped. "And left her alone?"

"She left her with Hart's boss."

What would become of the little girl if her father was

gone? Would she have to go to live in another country with a mother who had abandoned her?

Wendy's heart ached and a sense of urgency overcame her. Hart had been hired to protect her, but she needed to protect him. Not just for his sake but for his daughter's sake.

"I need to make sure he's okay," she murmured with a glance at his daughter, who'd fallen asleep on the couch.

"You can't go up there," her father said with an adamant shake of his gray-haired head. "It's not safe."

"I have to find Hart," Wendy said. "I have to make sure he's all right."

"And if he isn't?" her father asked. "What will you have done? Put yourself in danger for no reason."

Wendy pointed at the child. "She's not no reason. She's the best reason." Felicity needed her father.

"I'll go look for him," Wendy's father said as he reached for the gun in his waistband.

Her mother gasped and clutched at him.

Wendy shook her head. "No, Dad. I can't let you do that. This is all my fault."

"No, it's not," he assured her. "You were just doing your job."

She nodded in agreement. "A dangerous job that I'm trained to do. That's why I can go up there. You can't."

"Wendy…" Her mother reached for her, but Wendy stepped away.

She knew what she had to do. She had to find Hart. Fear gripped her, though, but it wasn't just fear for herself. She was afraid that, with all the gunfire, she would find him dead rather than alive.

"Casualties reported at a shooting in a residential neighborhood on the east side of River City," the radio report began in Parker Payne's SUV.

He shuddered. The moment Cole had called to report seeing movement around the Thompson home, Parker had known it wasn't good. That something bad was going to happen.

Just how bad?

Were any of those casualties from his team or Cooper's? He'd even sent in Logan's for backup, and most of his team was comprised of family members. But they might not have arrived in time.

He couldn't consider the other possibility: that those casualties might include civilians like Wendy Thompson's parents or a certain little girl.

He shouldn't have let her babysitter slip away like she had. Or better yet, after she had, Parker should have taken the child home with him. As a former nanny, his wife was awesome with kids.

But he knew the little girl had been missing her father and Winnie. Parker had figured she would be safe with Hart and Wendy and all the backup protecting the Thompson house.

Now his gut tightened into knots with tension and fear. Who the hell were the casualties?

As he drew closer to the block where the Thompsons lived, he saw the glow of lights. Police vehicles. SWAT vans. Ambulances...

News vehicles lined the side of the street, camera crews heading on foot toward the scene. A patrol car blocked the end of the road where he needed to turn. So he parked the SUV behind a news van and threw open his door.

And just as he did, he heard the sharp retort of gunfire. The attack was not over yet.

Chapter 12

Wendy heard the sirens and saw the lights flashing outside the broken windows of the home where she had grown up. Help had arrived. But it didn't sound as if they'd made their way inside yet. Police would not rush in with an active shooter until they were certain there was not a hostage situation.

There nearly had been one in the basement until Wendy had convinced her father that she had to do this. She had to find Hart and make certain he was okay.

He'd only gone, supposedly, to turn on the floodlight in the backyard. But she knew that if he'd seen something, he would have gone outside to investigate. He might have quit the River City PD, but a part of him would always be a detective.

She was acting like one now as she moved stealthily

through her parents' house, glass crunching under her feet. Despite it being dark, she could tell their home had been destroyed. She slid her hand over a wall until she flipped up a switch, but her father must have switched off a breaker because nothing happened.

There was no light but for the flickering flashes of the ones outside the house. As they flashed, she noticed a shadow moving through the dining room. She lifted her weapon just as that shadow swung a gun toward her.

He wasn't one of the bodyguards. In the flickering light, he looked barely older than the kids who'd come to their house for football team dinners. But he must have been old enough to work for Luther. Once he caught sight of her, he breathed a sigh of relief.

"There you are, bitch," he murmured.

Wendy tensed. She needed to pull the trigger. Needed to protect herself and the others. As she began to squeeze, a shot rang out.

She had acted too slowly. She closed her eyes and tensed even more, waiting for the pain to start. She'd heard so many people remark on how they hadn't realized in the moment that they'd been shot, that they hadn't felt it, maybe because of all the adrenaline.

Or they'd gone numb…

But Wendy wasn't numb. Her heart was pounding frantically. Her legs were shaking, but they had not folded beneath her. She was standing.

When she opened her eyes, in those flashes of light she saw that the kid was not standing. He'd fallen to the floor, his eyes open but his gaze blank. She gasped in shock.

Then another gun barrel glinted in the darkness. She raised her weapon. This time she would not hesitate.

Just as she began to squeeze the trigger, light flashed across the face of the shooter.

"Hart!" She jerked the barrel to the right so she wouldn't hit him. She also eased her finger off the trigger just in time, so she didn't actually fire at all. Her breath escaped in a ragged sigh. "Are you all right?"

He stepped forward and she saw the gun behind him—pointed directly at his back.

"Duck!" she yelled at him.

As he did, she fired, this time directly at his would-be assailant. But hers wasn't the only shot that rang out.

Had she pulled the trigger in time? Or had Hart been shot before she'd fired?

Hart was hurt. His chest ached with all the fear he'd felt for his daughter, for Wendy, and for himself and his fellow bodyguards. Lying on the floor, he whirled toward the person Wendy had fired at, but that kid was dead, like the one who'd tried to kill her.

She hadn't fired fast enough to protect herself, but she had to save him.

Why was he not surprised?

"Are you okay?" she asked.

He nodded and reached for his cell phone. The connection was open in another conference call between his boss and one of the perimeter guards.

"The house is secure now," he said.

Only two of Luther's crew had got past him and the

other Payne Protection bodyguards to make it into the house. And they both lay dead on the floor.

Some of them had died outside, as well. A few had had the sense to surrender before they'd been killed. But these two had been determined to carry out Luther's order to kill the evidence tech.

"Are you okay?" he asked her.

She nodded.

"And…" His chest ached with the fear that something might have happened to his little girl.

"She's fine," Wendy assured him then hurried away from him toward a steel door. She pounded on it and called out, "Dad, it's okay."

The scraping sound of dead bolts turning emanated from the door. Before it opened, there was another sound. A loud one as the front door burst open and men entered, guns drawn.

"Put down your weapons! Put down your weapons!" they shouted.

Hart lowered his to the floor but didn't completely release it. He nodded at Wendy to do the same. He didn't want one of the SWAT guys shooting her. "I said that the house is clear."

He narrowed his eyes as his heart began to pound hard again. Were they really SWAT guys? The black uniforms and bulletproof vests looked legit, and they wore their shields on chains around their necks. But even if they were really River City Special Response, it didn't mean they weren't part of Luther's crew.

He and Wendy and her parents, who must have been hiding behind that steel door with his daughter, weren't out of danger yet. "Don't open up yet!" he yelled out to Mr. Thompson.

"If they don't open it, we'll break it open," one of the guys threatened. "We need to secure the scene." Some of the other members of the SWAT team moved throughout the house, picking up weapons, checking pulses on the fallen gunmen.

But Hart didn't release the breath burning in his chest until Parker and the chief entered the house.

"Put your damn guns down," Chief Lynch told the SWAT members who still had barrels trained on Hart and Wendy.

The men quickly lowered their weapons and backed away.

"Are you all right?" Parker asked.

They both nodded.

Parker stepped closer to Hart and asked, "Is your daughter all right?"

Hart wanted to know that for himself. He started toward the door again. "Mr. Thompson, you can open it now."

A scream emanated from behind the door. A scream he recognized from her nightmares. A scream that gave him nightmares. He never wanted her to be as frightened as she must have been.

"It's okay, sweetheart," he called out to his baby just as the door began to open. "Everything's all right now, sweetheart."

Mr. Thompson pulled the door open all the way and stepped aside so Hart could join him on the small landing at the top of the stairs.

"Daddy, are you okay?" Felicity asked as she stared up at him from where Mrs. Thompson held her at the bottom of the stairs.

"I'm fine, honey," he replied with a sigh of relief. She looked unharmed.

"What about Winnie?" Felicity asked. "Is Winnie okay?"

Wendy joined him on the small landing. "I'm fine, honey," she replied with one of her forced smiles. It was clear that she was lying. She wasn't fine.

While she hadn't physically been harmed, her family home had been destroyed—her family put in danger, and she'd killed someone. That might have been the first time, as an evidence tech, that she'd even drawn her weapon. He knew that she wasn't fine because he wasn't fine, either. He was furious.

Luther Mills's crew never should have got close to the house, let alone inside it. Wendy and her family and his daughter should have been safe with all the protection they'd had.

But Luther had sent an army after them.

He was even more determined to kill Wendy than he had been to kill the eyewitness. Or maybe, since Rosie Mendez was out of his reach, Mills had focused all of his energy and resources on killing Wendy.

"You are not processing this crime scene," he told her, his voice pitched low.

The chief stood behind him, with Parker, and he must have been close enough to hear because he added, "Mr. Fisher is correct."

Hart wanted to get her and his daughter and Wendy's

parents out of the house. But he didn't want Felicity to see those bodies. So he motioned for Mrs. Thompson to stay at the bottom of the stairs for now.

Once the house had been cleared by the police, the paramedics were allowed to enter. They stopped at the bodies lying on the floor. But there was no help for them.

Had Wendy ever had to fire her weapon before? Was she all right? Or was she in shock? She must have been in shock because she wasn't fighting to process the scene.

More concern for her gripped Hart, and he grasped her arm, turning her toward him. "Are you really okay?"

She nodded again, but tears filled her eyes.

He felt a twinge in his heart and wanted to pull her into his arms and promise that he would keep her safe. But he had nearly failed her. Even he didn't know how he had survived the onslaught of bullets fired at him when he'd stepped out that back door.

Wendy's reddish lashes fluttered as she blinked furiously to clear the tears from her green eyes. "Yes," she said, pulling her arm from his grasp. "I am really okay."

Then she turned to the chief. "And even though I know that I legally can't, I wish I could process this scene. We need to find something that ties this assault to Luther Mills."

There was Hart's Wendy—ever determined to do her job. But he felt another twinge of panic at the possessive thought he'd just had. She was just his assignment. Nothing else. And after the dismal way he'd protected her, he probably wouldn't have this assignment much longer. He didn't even dare to look at his boss. Parker was probably furious with him.

The chief reached out to Wendy like Hart ached to do. He just squeezed her shoulder, though. "Ms. Thompson, don't worry about the crime scene or getting Luther Mills. Just worry about yourself and your family."

"I am," she said, her voice cracking. "I'm very worried about them."

Hart understood why. Because she'd nearly lost them. He, too, had been so afraid of what he would find inside the house—that he would find all of them dead.

Damn Luther Mills...

Some of the gunmen had survived the firefight; some had surrendered. The ones that hadn't had been overpowered by the ex-Marine bodyguards and Hart. He hoped at least one of them would talk—because Luther Mills's reign of terror needed to end.

Luther smirked as his lawyer entered the small conference room. The guy didn't look quite so slick now. He wasn't in one of his tailored suits. He wore a sweater and jeans, his hair was mussed, and his usually sharp eyes were bleary with sleep or maybe alcohol.

"What's so urgent? Why did you need to see me at this hour?" the lawyer asked, his voice gruff with irritation and weariness.

Luther's smirk slid into a grimace. If he wasn't able to sleep, why should his lawyer? The trial date was too close. And while he'd managed to get some comforts of the outside brought to him, the jail guards had got too nervous about smuggling in everything he wanted.

He had yet to get the eyewitness and another attempt to eliminate the damn evidence tech had just failed.

"I need you to represent some more clients for me," Luther said.

The lawyer balked. "You didn't…" He sighed. "I should have known."

He must have heard about the assault on the news. There had been casualties. Unfortunately, they had all been Luther's. Damn the Payne Protection Agency.

And especially Hart Fisher. Was it possible that Wendy Thompson was more than just a client to him?

How come these damn bodyguards couldn't keep it professional? he wondered. But then, it was personal to Luther, too. It was personal that he needed to take out the Payne Protection Agency along with everyone else associated with his damn trial.

They were all going down.

"You need to make sure these clients say that I didn't," Luther said. Because he suspected that hot assistant district attorney would do everything in her power to get his crew to talk. And it might not take much…

Some of them were out on bail from the previous attempts on the lives of Rosie Mendez and her damn bodyguard, Clint Quarters. They would be denied bail now. And they would be looking at long prison sentences.

Almost as long as the one Luther was looking at.

"They can't talk," he said. "You need to make that damn clear to them."

Or he would. He would make damn certain they weren't able to talk to anyone ever again. Maybe it had been a mistake to use that approach again.

The Payne Protection Agency had proved that it was able to withstand a bold, frontal attack. So maybe Luther needed to go about taking out the evidence tech another way—through a sneak attack that nobody, not even Hart Fisher, would see coming.

And if Hart got eliminated along with little Miss By-the-Book Wendy Thompson, then Luther would be damn happy.

Chapter 13

Her hands shook as she folded the sweater into the suitcase. Her mother reached out, putting her hand over Wendy's to steady it. "You're trembling."

She hadn't stopped—not since those first shots had rung out. She'd been so worried about Felicity. About her parents. About Hart…

And then having to shoot that kid…

But if she hadn't, Hart wouldn't have survived. A little girl would have lost the only parent she really had. Wendy's heart ached with regret for the fear the child had endured. For the fear her parents had endured.

"I'm so sorry, Mom," she murmured, and her voice vibrated with emotion. Tears rushed into her eyes again and she blinked, trying to clear them away. But one spilled over and ran down her cheek.

Like when she'd been a little girl, her mother gently brushed it from her face. Then she cupped Wendy's chin in her palm and assured her, "None of this was your fault."

Wendy shook her head. "Yes, it is my fault. I'm the reason the house got destroyed, why you and Dad nearly got killed."

Her father stepped out of the bathroom with another small bag, probably filled with toiletries. "We weren't nearly killed," he said. "And the house can be repaired. It was getting dated anyway. This'll give us a chance to do some long-overdue renovations."

Wendy couldn't hold back the tears now. They flowed as sobs slipped through her lips, too. Her father and mother both embraced her, like they had when she was little and needed comforting.

They had both always been there for her. Now, knowing that Felicity had only Hart, she realized how damn lucky she was. "I'm so sorry," she murmured again.

Her father drew back and cupped her face in his big hands. She felt the tremor in his fingers. He wasn't completely recovered from the attack yet, either. "None of this is your fault," he assured her like her mother just had. "It's that scumbag Luther Mills."

She nodded and he dropped his hands from her face.

"But you should have told us what was going on," he admonished.

The weight of the guilt already on her shoulders increased and she nodded again. "I'm sorry. But I didn't want to worry you."

"So you lied to us instead?" her father asked.

Heat rushed to her face. Her parents had punished her more any time she'd lied about her misbehavior growing up. When she'd been honest with them, she'd got in a lot less trouble. She should have been honest this time, too. Then she could have sent her parents away somewhere safe, where the chief and Parker Payne had promised to take them now.

"I'm sorry," she murmured again.

"You're not a good liar, Wendy," her father said. "We knew something was going on, and that worried us."

"I'm sorry I worried you," she said. "And I'm sorry for lying about my apartment and about Hart."

Her mother smiled and patted her cheek. "You weren't lying about him."

"He's not my boyfriend," Wendy insisted. "He's just my bodyguard."

Her mother and father exchanged a smile.

"That's all he is," she insisted and could hear the panic in her own voice.

Her mother's smile widened. "You've had a crush on him for a long time."

Too long. Her face heated even more over that sad, schoolgirl crush. "That was stupid."

"I don't think so, especially after meeting him," Margaret Thompson said with a wink.

Clearly, she and Wendy's father thought something more was going on between her and Hart, and she wasn't going to waste time arguing with them. Not when they needed to be taken off to that safe house.

"Are you finished packing?" she asked them.

Her mother chuckled at her change of subject.

"Do you have your stuff?" her father asked her.

She shook her head.

"You're going with us," he said as if it brooked no argument.

She wasn't a child anymore, even though her crush had made her look like one. "No, I'm not."

"But you're the one in danger," her mother said. "You have to come with us."

She shook her head again. "No. I can't *not* do my job. If I stop working, then Luther Mills wins before he even goes to trial."

"And if you die, he won't go to trial at all," a deep voice said.

She turned to find Hart leaning against the doorjamb. He had circles beneath his eyes that were even darker than his brown irises. His thick brown hair was mussed and his clothes were torn. A sleeve was ripped and his jeans were ragged at the knees.

He must have had to duck and dive to avoid being killed. How he had survived all those bullets, she couldn't fathom. But she was damn glad that he had. So glad that her heart filled with warmth.

Despite that, she opened her mouth to argue with him. Before she could say anything, though, a soft voice called out for him.

"Daddy…"

And he hurried away.

"Sure," her mother remarked. "He's just your bodyguard."

That was all he was.

Nothing more.

Wendy didn't even have a crush on him anymore. No. What she felt now for Hart Fisher went much deeper than a crush, but she had no doubt that it would be equally as unrequited.

Hart closed his arms around his daughter's tiny body and lifted her up against his chest. He loved her so damn much. If he'd lost her...

Felicity sighed as she settled her head against his shoulder. He'd only stepped away for a minute while she'd been in the bathroom. But she acted as if he'd been gone too long.

Could he spend any more time away from her? But he had to. He had to keep Wendy safe, especially since she was so damn stubborn.

"Everything's okay now, sweetheart," he assured her.

Felicity's head moved against his shoulder in a nod. "I know. It was just a game."

Wendy. Obviously she'd worked her magic with his daughter again to soothe her fears. She was amazing. Damn her.

He wanted to be furious with her. He wanted...

Her.

She stepped outside the den her parents had been using as their bedroom. She carried a suitcase, but he knew it wasn't hers. She'd made it clear she had no intention of joining them in the safe house.

Stubborn woman.

"Winnie!" Felicity exclaimed. She arched away from him, reaching for Wendy, who immediately dropped the suitcase and took the child from his arms.

Felicity hugged her tightly. How had a bond formed between them so quickly?

He saw the connection on Wendy's face, too. The love in her eyes just before she closed them. Felicity's own mother had never felt that kind of connection with her child.

But then, he suspected his ex didn't know how to give love; she only wanted to receive it. No. She didn't even know what love was—only infatuation. He pitied her new husband. From experience, he knew it wouldn't be long before Monica moved on to someone else.

"There's our princess!" Wendy's mother exclaimed as she limped out of the bedroom. But she wasn't talking about her daughter. She was talking about his.

Just as Felicity had arched away from him to reach for Wendy, she arched away from Wendy to reach for her mother. Before the shooting, she'd been shy with the older couple. But, enduring the ordeal together, she must have formed a bond with them, as well. She wrapped her arms around Margaret's neck and snuggled against her. "You smell like cookies."

"As soon as we get to our new house, we can bake some together," the older woman offered. "You can help me."

Hart tensed. "What?"

"We'd like to take her with us," Ben said, "if you're okay with that?"

He didn't know what to be with that. Offended they didn't think he could care for her? Relieved she would be safe and out of harm's way? Mostly he was just confused.

Wendy had told them the truth. They knew everything now.

"I don't understand…" he murmured.

And their daughter stared at them, her brow furrowed with confusion, too.

"We know about your childcare situation," Mrs. Thompson said.

That his babysitter had quit. He could find another one, though. Or he could take Parker's wife up on her previous offer to watch her. When Sharon had suggested it before, he'd thought he had everything under control. He'd been wrong, though.

Tonight had proved that. He'd put his own child in danger. His stomach churned as he felt sick over it.

He would have never forgiven himself.

"But still," he said. "You know that I'm not really…" He glanced at Wendy, whose face flushed nearly as red as her hair over the awkwardness of their situation.

"I'm going to talk to the chief before he leaves," she murmured and then hurried down the hall away from them.

She was probably going to make another argument for working the crime scene. Or for continuing to work despite everyone's arguments that she needed to go to that safe house, too.

She was the one in the most danger. But tonight his child had been in danger, as well. Her parents were offering him a way to keep her safe.

"We know *what* you really are," Margaret said, but she was smiling. Maybe for his daughter's sake. The little girl was staring up at her.

"Then why…?" Hart asked.

Her mother took Felicity aside as her father stepped closer and lowered his voice. "You're protecting our daughter. Let us protect yours."

Hart blinked. He'd thought the Paynes were a unique family, how they accepted outsiders and made them feel like family. But the Thompsons were a hell of a lot like them. They were making him and his daughter feel like family.

He could hear Mrs. Thompson asking his daughter, "Would you like to go on vacation with me and Papa Ben while your daddy and Winnie work?"

The little girl nodded eagerly in agreement. And the tightness in Hart's chest eased. She was comfortable with Wendy's parents, more comfortable than she'd ever been with her own mother.

Ben pitched his voice lower and added, "We're going to have an army of bodyguards and we're going to be in a very safe location. She'll be protected with us."

Hart had thought she would be safe tonight, too. But Luther's crew had got close. Too close.

The chief and Parker had assured them all, though, that the Thompsons would be somewhere that nobody but their bodyguards would know about. There would be no way for Luther's mole to get him the information about their whereabouts.

"Are you sure?" Hart asked. "Her babysitter quit…" Felicity wasn't a difficult child, but she'd been through a lot and had trouble connecting with people. Of course, she hadn't had any trouble connecting with any of the Thompsons.

Ben chuckled. "My wife was a kindergarten teacher and I was a coach until our recent retirement. We've never met a kid we couldn't handle." His brow creased momentarily. "Except maybe our own…"

Hart chuckled now. He could understand that, since their child was Wendy. His amusement faded. "She should be going with you."

"She won't." Her father apparently knew and accepted that, whereas Hart still wanted to fight with her about it.

Hell, he just wanted her.

Ben reached out, planting a beefy hand on Hart's shoulder, and he nearly jumped. Had the older man read his mind?

"You keep Wendy safe," Ben said. "She's a stubborn one—determined to keep working."

Damn her. She was stubborn. Too damn stubborn. And it was probably going to get her killed.

He could trust the Thompsons with his child. But he wasn't so sure they should trust him with theirs.

Woodrow Lynch had daughters of his own, even more now that he'd married Penny Payne. Her children were his and vice versa. They also tended to collect other people's children as theirs. He felt very paternal toward Wendy Thompson. He cared about her so much that, like his own children, she managed to frustrate the hell out of him.

Over the body bags of the men who'd nearly killed her, she pleaded with him to let her continue working—without a bodyguard, of course.

Or, at least, without Hart Fisher.

She turned to Parker, who stood beside Woodrow. "He needs to be with his daughter. She could have died tonight." As she said it, her voice cracked with emotion. The child meant something to her.

"Go with your parents," Woodrow urged her. "Go into protective custody until after the trial. Your job will wait."

She shook her head. "No, it can't. You're the one who told me about those other cases against Luther falling apart. If I go missing, the evidence might go missing, as well."

He winced. But he couldn't argue with her. Getting rid of Wendy made no sense because the evidence would still exist. Unless Luther already had a plan in place for someone to destroy the evidence once Wendy was out of the way.

Someone like another crime scene investigator.

But if Wendy had someone within her own department whom she couldn't trust, she was in even more danger than the chief had feared. She wouldn't be safe anywhere.

But that safe house.

If she was gone, he had a horrible feeling that the evidence would disappear, too, because someone else would have to know where it was to ensure the chain of custody. Someone who might already be on Luther's payroll.

He couldn't risk that, so he had no choice but to risk her life instead.

Chapter 14

Wendy had won her argument to continue working on other cases while she waited for the trial. But she hated the reason why: that there was someone within the police department she couldn't trust. Someone working for a murderer.

She shivered.

Hart reached out and turned up the heat so that warm air blasted out of the vents of the SUV. She hadn't won the argument for him to be removed as her bodyguard, though. She was surprised that she was the only one who thought he shouldn't protect her. Being around her put him in too much danger, just as it had her family and his daughter.

"Where are you taking me?" she asked.

"Someplace safe," he said.

She tensed. "You better not take me anywhere near that safe house where my parents and Felicity are going."

He glanced across at her. "I don't even know where they're going."

She closed her eyes as regret overwhelmed her. "I'm sorry," she murmured. "That must be hard—to not know where your daughter is being taken."

"I know she will be safe," he said. "And that's most important."

Wendy couldn't argue with that. But she kept her eyes closed as tears continued to burn behind them.

"She will also be with very good people," he said, his deep voice gruff with emotion. "Your parents are so good with her."

The SUV stopped. And a door opened.

Wendy opened her eyes just as Hart rounded the front of the SUV and opened her door. "We're here," he said.

She looked around now and recognized the street in the old warehouse district of River City. It was slowly being transformed to a residential area since some of the warehouses had been converted to industrial-style condos. But yellow tape hung from some of the light poles.

She looked back at Hart and said, "This is a crime scene."

She had been called out to process the scene. In the past week, there had been a shoot-out here when Luther's crew had tried to take out Rosie Mendez. Just as had happened at her home, some of Luther's crew had died here.

But that didn't mean they wouldn't return.

"Why would you bring me here?" she asked.

"Because I live here," Hart said.

"You bought the safe house?"

He shook his head. "No. I live in this condo." He pointed to one on the other side of the street. It didn't look much different than a warehouse from the front. Some brick had been added to the metal, and a brick sidewalk led to a heavy steel front door. It looked quite similar to the Payne safe house condo.

"I just bought it a couple months ago when it was completed," he said. "There's a courtyard in the middle of the building with a playground."

He'd bought the place for Felicity. And now he didn't even know where his daughter was.

Too overwhelmed with guilt to argue with him, she let him guide her to the front door. He opened it quickly and ushered her inside. Then he closed and locked the heavy steel door behind them.

"There," he said. "We're safe."

Wendy didn't feel safe, not alone with him in his home. And it was a home. Toys sat out on a table in front of the couch, as if they'd been playing but had to leave before they'd finished.

Felicity shouldn't have had to leave her home and father because of her.

"I'm sorry," she said again.

"That you didn't go into protective custody, too?" he asked, a dark brow arching.

She shook her head. "I'm sorry that I put you and Felicity in danger."

"You didn't," he said. "Luther Mills did."

"I tried to get Parker to take you off this assignment,

to let you go with my parents and Felicity..." She felt an ache in her chest at the thought of being separated from the little girl, and she'd just met her. She couldn't imagine how much he hurt over the separation.

Instinctively she reached out, placing her palm on his chest. His heart pounded heavily beneath her hand. "You don't want me protecting you anymore?" he asked.

"I don't want to put you or your daughter in danger," she said. "Or my parents..." She closed her eyes as tears rushed up again. She was too exhausted to control her emotions. She couldn't remember the last time she'd had a full night's sleep. She certainly hadn't had one since the threats had started.

"Your parents are safe," he said, his deep voice soft as if she were a little girl whose fears he was trying to soothe. "Felicity is safe."

She opened her eyes. "You're not." She could remember that gun pointed at him, that kid nearly killing him. And she cringed.

"No, I'm not," he agreed with a heavy sigh. "I'm not safe at all."

He was looking at her like she was the threat, not Luther Mills.

Then he lowered his head and covered her mouth with his. He kissed her tenderly at first, just skimming his lips back and forth over hers.

She gasped at a rush of desire, and he deepened the kiss. His tongue slid in and out of her mouth as he tasted her. Then he groaned.

Suddenly she was being lifted and carried. She clutched at him. Not so that she wouldn't fall.

She knew it was too late for that. She'd already fallen for Hart Fisher.

Even before he'd saved her life over and over.

She was helpless to fight her feelings any longer. She was helpless to fight the passion that overpowered her. She'd nearly lost him, nearly lost her opportunity to ever be this close to him. When he set her on a bed, she clung to him, pulling him down on top of her like he'd been that night he'd sneaked into her room.

Their legs tangled and she felt the evidence of his passion as his erection rubbed against her hip. She moaned and arched against him.

"Wendy…" he murmured as he tried to ease back, away from her.

She might have let him go, if she hadn't seen the desire on his face, which was flushed, his eyes glittering. He wanted her, too.

She moved her hand between them, across the erection that pushed against the fly of his worn jeans. His breath hissed out between his clenched teeth.

"You're killing me," he murmured.

She shook her head. "No. I don't want that to happen. I want you…"

Alive.

Right now she wanted him period. Any way she could have him. And in this moment, she was glad his boss and hers had refused to remove him as her bodyguard.

While he might never be her boyfriend, tonight or this morning as it was, he could be her lover. She reached for the button on his jeans.

He jerked back. "Slow down," he cautioned between pants for breath.

Slow down.

Not stop.

He wanted her, too.

She smiled and lay back on the bed. His bed. The room was dark: dark walls, dark blinds, dark trim. Even his sheets and blankets were dark; a rich chocolate brown like his eyes. But his eyes weren't brown as he stared down at her. They turned black, the pupils completely dilated with desire.

She yanked up her shirt, pulled it over her head and tossed it onto the floor. Her bra wasn't particularly sexy. She didn't own any lace or silk. Lace was scratchy and silk felt cold. She preferred cotton, but it was a deep green, and her breasts swelled over the cups as she breathed heavily.

He groaned again. "Wendy..."

Then she reached for his shirt, tugging it up over his washboard abs that rippled when she brushed her knuckles across them.

He sucked in a breath, as if she'd slugged him. But then he dragged off the shirt and his holster. The gun went on a table next to the bed, the shirt with hers on the floor. They moved quickly then, both discarding their pants. His underwear went with his, leaving him completely naked and perfect.

He was so muscular. So fit.

Wendy's curves were a little too soft. But he didn't seem to mind when his erection pressed against her again. He lowered himself onto her, kissing her lips before sliding his mouth along her throat. His tongue flicked over her leaping pulse. Then he moved farther down her body.

He unclasped the bra and tugged it away to free her breasts. Then he slid his mouth across them, over the mound of flesh, before closing his lips around a nipple. He pulled on it gently.

She cried out as pleasure rushed through her. Desire pounded in her core, which ached for him. She needed him like she'd never needed anyone before.

She reached out and closed her fingers around his shaft. He was so long, so thick. She moved her hand up and down the length of him.

He groaned. "I'll go too soon," he warned her as he pulled away from her touch.

"I don't care," she murmured. She needed him now. She needed him fast.

"But I want to please you," he said as he moved farther down the bed, down her body. Her underwear disappeared just as quickly as her bra had.

Was she dreaming? She must be dreaming.

But it felt so real—when he kissed her intimately, when he moved his mouth over her core. She arched and cried out as a small orgasm rushed through her. She nearly sobbed that it wasn't enough. She wanted more. So much tension gripped her yet. She grasped his broad shoulders, trying to tug him up.

But he pulled away. And she heard something tear. Then she watched as he rolled a condom over his shaft.

She parted her legs for him and helped guide him into her. He was so big, she had to arch, had to shift to take him deeper.

Then he moved inside her and that tension built even more, threatening to break her apart. She whimpered and moaned.

"Are you okay?" he asked, his voice gruff with passion and concern. "I'm not too…"

Perfect. That was what she'd always thought he was. Now she knew she'd been right.

He fit her perfectly. She moved beneath him, arching and stretching to take him even deeper, and he groaned.

He lowered his head and kissed her, deeply, passionately. Their mouths mated like their bodies. Then his hands moved between their bodies, over her breasts, teasing the nipples…

She moaned into his mouth.

He moved his one hand lower, flicking a finger across the most sensitive part of her body. And she came and came…crying out his name as the pleasure overwhelmed her.

His body tensed and, with a loud groan, he found his release, as well.

Wendy had never been as satiated or as scared as she lay there in Hart Fisher's bed, in Hart Fisher's arms. She was afraid of Luther Mills and the people who worked for him.

But she was also afraid of her feelings. She was afraid that she had fallen deeply and irrevocably in love with Hart.

* * *

Hart had been in some dangerous situations before. Hell, he'd thought the most dangerous one had been at her parents' home when he'd come under all that gunfire in the backyard. But now he knew this was dangerous, too. Wendy Thompson was dangerous—to him.

He'd lost his focus and had allowed his desire for her to distract him from his job. It wasn't to make love to her; it was to protect her.

But now he felt like he needed protection. From her...

He'd come back to bed, though, after cleaning up. And he'd slid his arms around her and pulled her naked body against his. She was so warm and soft.

She slept as if she'd passed out. Maybe she had. He'd nearly fainted from the pleasure she'd given him. He couldn't remember ever feeling so much passion and such a powerful release. His body had shuddered. It shuddered even now as he remembered...

Then a certain part of his body reacted. He wanted her all over again. But he couldn't disturb her.

He didn't know the last time she'd slept. From the dark circles beneath her eyes, he suspected it had been a while. Her lashes, which were nearly as red as her hair, lay over those circles. And that sprinkle of freckles across her nose and cheeks tempted him to touch.

She was so damn cute. Her hair had tangled around her face. But it was soft against his skin. Just like she was...

Soft and warm and sweet.

How hadn't he noticed her before? Sure, he knew

they'd worked together. He remembered getting teased that she'd had a crush on him. But he'd been married part of that time. Not that it had been a happy marriage.

From the first, he'd realized it was a mistake. But with Felicity already on the way, he'd wanted to try to make it work. After the marriage had failed, the last thing he'd wanted was to ever try that again with anyone.

Wendy seemed like the type of woman who wanted a commitment. She probably wanted a marriage like her parents had. But she had no way of knowing how rare and special that was. Hart knew and, because he did, he wasn't going to risk looking for something that elusive.

No. Making love to her had been a mistake. But when she'd touched his chest, his heart, he'd been unable to stop the rush of desire that had overwhelmed him. He'd needed her like he'd needed air.

Air.

He needed that now, because every time he breathed, he inhaled her sweet scent and the scent of their passion, until his lungs filled with it. He needed air. But when he tried to slide his arm out from underneath her, she murmured in protest.

"Shh," he said. "I'll be right back."

"Where are you going?" she asked, suddenly fully awake.

"Just going to check outside," he said. "I want to make sure all my backup is in place." He'd told Parker where he was taking her. But neither of them had thought he'd need many other bodyguards.

Luther was unlikely to find enough men to stage another attack so quickly. Hell, most of his crew was either in jail or the morgue right now.

Too bad Luther couldn't join them.

"I'll be fine," Hart assured her.

She clutched at him. It wasn't like she had earlier, with passion. It was with fear. "You remember what happened last time you checked outside."

He'd nearly been killed. He didn't need the reminder. But he still needed the air. He pulled her hands from his arms. "I will be fine," he said again. Then he shared with her what he and Parker had already deduced. "Luther is using up his crew. They're dying or going to jail. He can't have that many more to send after us—at least, not so soon."

She stared up at him for a long moment. "If that's what you think, then why do you need to check on your backup? Why do you need backup?"

She knew. He wasn't going outside for her protection. He was going outside for his.

Doubt nagged at Parker, along with that sick certainty that something bad was about to happen. It already nearly had the night before. But everyone had survived. So why hadn't the feeling gone away?

Because Wendy Thompson had refused to...

She wouldn't go to the safe house with her parents and Hart's daughter. The chief should have ordered her to do it. To go away...

But could they be certain she would be safe anywhere?

Luther had to be even more determined to take her out than he'd been the eyewitness.

Wendy had collected all the evidence that proved him guilty beyond the shadow of any doubt. She had to stay alive to keep it safe and keep the chain of custody of that evidence unbroken. Once she turned it over to someone else, there was a very real possibility that it would disappear. That feeling nagging at him, he picked his cell up from his desk and tapped Hart's contact number.

This time his bodyguard actually answered on the first ring, which was probably a good sign. If he was busy getting shot at, he wouldn't have had the time to answer.

"Everything okay?" Parker asked.

Hart's long hesitation had his heart pounding hard and fast.

"Is everything okay?" he asked again.

"Yeah, yeah," Hart replied, but he sounded distracted.

"Are you?" Parker asked. He'd been separated from his child. Maybe Wendy had been right. Maybe he should have sent Hart off with her parents and his daughter.

There was another long hesitation.

"What's going on?" Parker demanded.

Before Hart could say anything more, a blast reverberated from the phone. It wasn't a gunshot. It was louder than that. Like an explosion.

Parker remembered that sound well from when he'd nearly been blown up a few years ago.

"Hart? Hart!" he called out.

There was no reply. Parker wasn't even sure if the cell phone was still working or if it—and Hart—had been destroyed in the explosion.

Chapter 15

The windows rattled and the old warehouse structure shook from the force of the explosion. It was close. Too close.

Wendy had dressed after Hart had left the bed. She hadn't been able to sleep without him. Now she grasped her gun and headed to where he'd gone. Outside.

He should have listened to her that it was too dangerous. But he'd seemed determined, or even desperate, to get away from her, probably because he'd regretted what they'd done.

She didn't, even though she would undoubtedly wind up having her heart broken. Her only regret was not forcing him to stay in bed with her.

"Hart!" she called, her heart beating frantically with fear.

When she stepped into the living room, she saw the

glow of a fire outside the front window. The SUV Hart had parked at the curb was fully engulfed in flames.

Where was Hart?

Gripping her weapon tightly in one hand, she unlocked and opened the door with the other. Of course, Hart had locked her in; he wanted to keep her safe even while he kept putting himself in danger.

"Hart!" she called again. She tried to get closer to the SUV, but the heat of the flames was overwhelming. Was he inside?

He wouldn't have got in it. He wouldn't have left her.

"Hart!" Panic gripped her now, pressing so hard on her chest that she could barely draw a breath.

Black smoke roiled off the flames consuming the burning vehicle, turning day into night. She couldn't see anything. But she had to get closer, had to find Hart.

As she moved forward, she bumped into someone also moving around in the smoke. "Hart!" she exclaimed.

But the grasp on her arm was too tight, too painful to be his. For a moment, the smoke cleared and she could see the face of the man holding on to her.

It wasn't Hart's handsome face. This man's features were cruder and swollen, like he'd been in quite a few fights in his lifetime. And he was older. At least, older than the kids who usually worked for Luther.

He wasn't anyone she recognized. But she recognized the look in his cold, dark eyes. Even though she didn't know who he was, she knew what he was.

A killer.

Had he already killed Hart?

* * *

The force of the blast had knocked Hart to the ground. And the sound of it roared in his ears. So he couldn't hear anything but it right now.

And through the thick smoke, he could barely see. So he wasn't sure how he knew—but he just knew—that Wendy was in danger.

Of course, the explosion had probably been a distraction, intended to draw him outside, away from her. But Hart had already been outside when the SUV had exploded. He'd already been distracted.

He knew the explosion would have drawn her outside, as well.

The wind picked up, clearing the smoke for a moment. And he saw them: the big man who held tightly on to Wendy. A protest scorched Hart's throat as his lungs burned with smoke. He pushed himself off the pavement, lurching to his feet. His entire body shook.

He grabbed for his weapon. But his holster was empty. The gun must have been knocked out when he'd fallen. Where the hell was it?

Wendy had her gun, though.

And now he knew she wouldn't hesitate to use it. Or maybe because she had used it once already—and taken a life—she would hesitate before turning the barrel toward the man who held on to her.

The man tightened his grasp, though, bending her arms so the gun wouldn't point toward him. Then he reached for it.

If he got it away from her…

If he turned it on her…

Hart propelled his body forward, launching himself at the man like the explosion had launched him into the air. His back to Hart, the man hadn't seen him coming.

The attack took him down but knocked Wendy over, also. She lay sprawled beneath the weight of two men.

Hart wrapped his arm around the guy's neck, trying to choke him. But the guy reared up and shook him off as if he was just a child trying to get a piggyback ride. And, at the moment, Hart felt as weak as a child, as if the explosion had zapped all his muscles.

He dropped to the ground again.

When the man turned and reached out gloved hands to grab him, they both heard the cocking of Wendy's weapon. The man tensed, as if still considering grabbing Hart. But then he ran, jumping over him in his haste to escape a bullet.

She had saved his life again, just as she had at her parents' house.

Which one of them was the real bodyguard? He certainly felt as if she'd protected him more than he had her.

"Are you okay?" she asked as she stood over him. Her face was tight and pale with fear and concern.

All the breath had been knocked from his burning lungs again, so he just nodded.

"What the hell happened?" she asked. "Why would someone blow up your SUV?"

He had to admit that it didn't seem like something Luther Mills would order. But then, neither had cutting someone's brake line.

Luther was never that subtle.

Of course, there was nothing subtle about an explosion. Since his hearing had returned, Hart was aware of the whine of sirens in the distance. And the deep rumble of other male voices.

His backup had arrived.

Lars Ecklund, one of Cooper's team, rushed up. The giant of a man reached down and lifted Hart to his feet as if he weighed no more than Felicity's treasured rag doll. "You okay?" he asked. The ex-Marine looked pale, and it probably wasn't just because his hair and eyes were so light. It was probably because the explosion had brought him war flashbacks.

Hart felt like he was in the middle of a war right now himself. A war to protect Wendy.

"I'm fine," he said. But he wasn't. He was worried as hell—about her.

Luther had obviously stepped up his attempts. He was going after her even more relentlessly than he'd gone after Rosie Mendez. Hart and Parker had been wrong; it hadn't taken Luther very long to send someone else after her.

How the hell had he found them so quickly, though? Had he followed them from her parents' house to Hart's condo?

Hart had watched the rearview fanatically again. But he had missed that white van before. Was this guy the driver of that van?

It made sense that he would be older. One of the kids from the earlier attack on the Thompson house wouldn't have been able to tail Hart undetected the way this guy had.

"What about you?" Lars asked her. "Are you okay, Ms. Thompson?"

She nodded. But she looked afraid.

Hart couldn't blame her.

He'd put himself in dangerous situations before, but he'd never had anyone as determined to kill him as Luther Mills was determined to kill Wendy. He wasn't sure how the hell he was going to keep her safe.

"I need to preserve as much of this scene as I can," she told Lars. "I need to figure out what kind of explosives and detonator were used."

Feeling like a broken record again, Hart told her, "You are not processing this damn crime scene. You can't, since it's yours."

She stared at him, or perhaps she stared through him. All of her attention was on the burned-out vehicle behind him. "It doesn't make sense that it was yours…"

"Yours isn't here," Hart pointed out. "He couldn't blow up what wasn't here. And I'm sure he just planted the bomb to draw us outside."

Lars nodded in agreement. "A diversion…"

"That's one hell of a diversion," she remarked. "It drew everyone's attention."

That was true. If the guy had hoped to escape without being seen, he should have gone with a smaller explosion, not one that must have been heard and felt for blocks. But since there was nothing subtle about Luther Mills, the bomb must have been his doing.

Wendy looked skeptical, though, her teeth nipping into her bottom lip as she studied the area. While she didn't touch anything so as not to compromise evidence, she carefully inspected the scene.

"That's one cool chick," Lars Ecklund remarked. "And I know cool chicks."

He was married to Parker Payne's sister. Nikki was a bodyguard herself. She was also a computer genius.

Yes, Wendy did have quite a bit in common with the resourceful, tough Nikki Payne-Ecklund.

But was it enough to keep her from getting killed?

"An explosion..." the chief murmured as he rubbed his head. It hurt as if he'd been there, as if he had felt the blast himself.

"Doesn't sound like Luther Mills, does it?" Parker remarked.

"I think we've only scratched the surface of what that man is capable of." And who he was capable of manipulating to carry out his wishes. Woodrow stared through his office window into the detectives' bull pen.

Wendy was there, with Hart, giving her statement about everything that had transpired. Was one of those detectives working with Mills?

Who all had he got to? This had been a professional hit. Or a hit staged by a professional, like a lawman or maybe an evidence tech...

If an evidence technician could put a device back together after it had detonated, that tech could probably put one together before it had detonated in the first place.

Just who the hell had Luther sent to take out Wendy Thompson? And would Parker and his bodyguards find that person in time to save her?

Chapter 16

Wendy slammed the book of mug shots closed. Flipping through them was a waste of time that would have been better spent processing the evidence that had been collected at the scene. But she couldn't touch it. From what she'd observed, though, the bomb had been sophisticated. Too sophisticated for one of Luther's young crew to have assembled.

But she'd got a good look at the guy. And she knew he was not one of Luther's usual minions.

Detective Spencer Dubridge pushed another book toward her. But she shoved it back across his messy desk. "I already told you that I didn't recognize him."

"That's why you need to look through the books," he pointed out. "To see if you can find him."

"If he was in any of these books, I would have recognized him."

Hart snorted. "Like you know every mug shot in those books."

Wendy had a photographic memory. But that wasn't something she shared with many people. She was especially good at facial recognition.

"When I started receiving those threats, I looked up all of Luther's known associates," she said.

Dubridge nodded. "That was smart, so you would notice if one of them approached you." He glanced over to where his blonde bodyguard sat in a chair at another detective's desk. "Makes a bodyguard unnecessary."

Wendy couldn't argue that hers wasn't necessary. Hart had saved her too many times. But her bodyguard didn't have to be Hart. In fact, she would feel much better if it was anyone but him, especially after what they'd done…to each other.

She couldn't even look at him now without blushing. Ignoring him, she persisted. "If that guy was one of Luther's crew, I would have recognized him."

"Pretty much all of Luther's *known* associates are either locked up," Detective Dubridge said, "for the shootings. Or dead."

"Then it was probably an officer or evidence tech," Hart said. Obviously he didn't care anymore if Luther's mole knew they were onto him or her.

"I would have recognized an officer or an evidence tech," she pointed out defensively.

"So he hired some outside talent," Hart suggested.

"Maybe he doesn't trust his own guys to get the job done anymore."

"He has every reason to trust them," a female voice said.

The assistant district attorney, Jocelyn Gerber, walked into the bull pen, her heels clicking against the terrazzo flooring. "Not a damn one of them will turn on him, not even to save himself from a long jail sentence."

"Maybe they figure it's better to be in jail than dead," her bodyguard, Landon Myers, remarked.

Despite how close he stood to her, Jocelyn ignored him as if he hadn't spoken and focused on Wendy instead. "That's why we need the guy who planted that bomb," she said. "If he's not one of Luther's regular crew, he might not have any loyalty or fear of him."

Wendy shivered as she remembered the cold look in the man's dark eyes. "I can work with a sketch artist on a drawing of him," she said. "Maybe it'll come up in someone else's database."

Jocelyn nodded. "Good." But she didn't sound hopeful.

If Luther Mills had an inkling that this guy might turn on him, he'd probably already ordered him killed. Their only hope of taking down the desperate drug dealer was for the murder for which he was supposed to stand trial soon.

Wendy had the evidence that would prove his guilt. She just had to stay alive to preserve it.

Hart hadn't needed the ADA taking him aside at River City PD to explain how important Wendy was to her case. He already knew how important Wendy was.

With every moment he spent with her, she became more and more important to him. He'd lost his professionalism when he'd made love with her. But he hadn't lost his objectivity.

He knew he had to keep her alive. But it wasn't just for Jocelyn Gerber and her damn case. He had to keep her alive because he couldn't imagine a world without Wendy Thompson in it.

While he knew they had no future, he wanted her to have one, with a nice guy who wasn't damaged like he was. Who still believed in love and happily-ever-after...

He wanted that for her. He also wanted her.

So damn badly that his hands shook as he swiped the card through the lock of the hotel room door. Taking her to a hotel felt romantic, like they were a couple enjoying a special getaway together.

The only thing they were getting away from were the people who wanted to kill Wendy.

Hart had had nowhere else to take her. The local safe houses had all been compromised. That was how he knew his daughter and Wendy's parents weren't anywhere near River City.

And knowing that let him breathe a little easier. At least his little girl was safe. He had no doubt that Wendy's parents would keep her happy and healthy. They would take good care of her, just as they had their own daughter.

Now he had to take care of her—to make sure she stayed safe, even from him. He had to make sure that he didn't inadvertently break her heart.

"I wish I was in the police lab," Wendy said. "I wish I was working the evidence from the explosion."

"You can't process your own crime scene, and you're not the only one who can process evidence," he reminded her.

"Even the chief suspects that there's a leak in the lab," she said on a ragged sigh of frustration. "He thinks that another tech helped evidence against Mills for previous crimes disappear."

"Do you believe it?" he asked. He knew she'd struggled to accept that anyone within her department could be working for Luther Mills.

But her illusions must have been shattered after all the attempts on her life because she grimly nodded.

"I'm sorry," he said. "It must be hard to think someone you work with could betray you."

She nodded again then uttered another ragged sigh. "You must feel the same way."

"Nobody at Payne Protection would betray me," he said with utter confidence. All the Paynes were too good judges of character. They wouldn't hire someone who was capable of betrayal.

"I meant someone you used to work with," she said. "The chief thinks more people than that rookie cop are working for Luther. That other officers or detectives could be, as well."

Hart chuckled. "I worked at RCPD when all the corruption was still going on within the station. We knew there were bad cops then. And it was never clear if every one of them had been caught."

"Apparently they haven't been."

He hated seeing her like this, so bitter and disillusioned. Maybe she was just tired, though. While she'd slept in his arms, she hadn't slept long.

"You should get some rest," he said.

She glanced over at the bed. There was only one. But the single had been the only room available in the hotel just outside River City. Autumn was popular for color tours in Michigan. The hotel must have been booked solid with travelers. Maybe he should have picked another one.

"I'm going to watch the door," he said. Or watch her sleep.

And remember what it had been like to touch her, to taste her.

His body tensed as desire gripped him.

"You must be tired, too," she said. "You couldn't have slept much if at all…"

She'd fallen asleep after they'd made love, so she wouldn't know that he'd been awake the entire time. Worried…

Not just about her but about making love with her. He could not fall for her, not after what he'd gone through. His heart was too messed up. But her…

She had to know that he wasn't the guy for her. She deserved someone as hopeful and optimistic as she was.

"I didn't sleep," he admitted with a heavy sigh. He needed to apologize for what had happened, for how he'd crossed the line. But when he opened his mouth to do that, she pressed her fingers over his lips.

"Don't," she said. "Please, don't…"

"Wendy—"

"Please," she implored again. "You're going to make me feel like a bigger idiot than I already do."

"I'm the idiot," he insisted. "I'm supposed to be protecting you. And I took advantage—"

She laughed.

"What?" he asked. "I did."

She snorted. "I took advantage," she said. "I wanted you. I wanted to do that."

He felt a twinge of regret. He was going to hurt her, and that was the last thing he wanted to do. "I know you had a crush on me in the past."

She snorted again. "Lust," she said. "That's what I felt. That's what I acted on."

Now his face heated with embarrassment. She'd just lusted after him?

She shrugged. "It's no big deal. We'd just been through a hell of a firefight. Having sex was just a way of reminding myself that we survived, that we were alive."

He narrowed his eyes and studied her face. Was she really that okay with what had happened?

She held up her palms. "I really have no expectations," she assured him.

He felt a strange twinge in his chest. But it must have been relief. She sounded sincere. So sincere that he wasn't worried about hurting her.

"That's good," he said, "because I've been married once and that's something I'm never going to do again."

She exhaled a heavy breath. "I'm not proposing to you. And I'm not expecting you to propose, either. I know that what happened between us just happened in the heat of the moment and that it won't happen again."

"You're wrong," he said as he hooked his arm around her waist and dragged her up against his hard, needy body. Since she didn't want anything from him but sex, he could give in to the desire he felt for her. "It's going to happen again."

She stared up at him, her green eyes wide with surprise. But her lips curved into a smile. A seductive one. "Oh, you think it is?"

"I know it is," he assured her, and he lowered his head, kissing her deeply.

Her arms linked around his neck as she kissed him back just as passionately. Their tongues mated and they panted for breath.

His gut twisted as desire fiercely gripped him. He had never felt like this before, had never wanted anyone as much. "Wendy…"

It was a mistake. Just as it had been before. He needed to focus on protecting her, not on the passion between them. But that passion was too hot to be denied.

They undressed quickly. He wasn't sure who removed what. She was as desperate for him as he was for her.

They fell onto the bed, a tangle of naked arms and legs. She moved on top of him, pressing her lips to his chest and his stomach before moving lower. Her mouth slid over his erection and he nearly came.

But that wasn't what he wanted. He wanted to be inside her again, so close that it felt as if they became one person. He tumbled her onto her back and reached over the bed, fishing a condom from his jeans.

She took the packet from his hand and tore it open with her teeth. Then she rolled it over the length of him. He gritted his teeth, but a groan still slipped through. He wanted to thrust inside her—deep. But he needed to make sure she was ready for him. So he pushed her onto her back again and he moved his mouth over her body. He used his tongue to tease a nipple into a tight point. Then he moved lower and swiped his tongue across the most sensitive part of her.

When he touched her with his fingers, he found her ready. Hot and wet. She arched against his hand and cried as she came. She was that responsive. That incredible.

That greedy. She pushed him onto his back now and climbed on top of him, easing him inside her. He groaned again as he slid deep. Then she lifted herself up and nearly off him before coming down again.

Then she rocked.

And drove him out of his mind, to the brink of madness. He gripped her hips and together they found a rhythm. She matched his thrusts and his urgency. They went wild in each other's arms. Then she tensed and screamed his name as her inner muscles gripped him and convulsed as she came.

He tensed right before the peak, the soul-shattering relief that had him pumping his hips as if he was filling her. Something filled him, flooded his heart. But he refused to let it stay.

Just as he didn't stay in bed with her. He hurried

into the bathroom to clean up and splash cold water on his face, hoping it would bring him to his damn senses. He hadn't just lost his objectivity. He'd lost his mind, as well.

His mind he could afford to lose, though. His heart was what he would never risk again. He sucked in a steadying breath before stepping back into the room with her.

Fortunately, she'd pulled up the sheets to cover herself. But he knew she wasn't sleeping this time. Her body was too tense.

Had he hurt her?

Had she been lying when she'd claimed to have no expectations? Was she really okay that it was just sex?

His cell rang, saving him from having to say anything to her. Maybe one of the bodyguards who'd followed them had heard her screams and wanted to make sure she was okay. Heat rushed to his face.

They would all know that he'd crossed the line.

"Hart, Nikki here," the female Payne bodyguard greeted him. "You said that was a white van that tried running you over and then off the road later?"

"Yes," he said.

"I found it on the surveillance footage from the cameras outside the department."

"You got access to that?" Of course, Chief Lynch was her stepfather, so he might have willingly given it to her. But he'd also heard that she was quite the hacker, as well.

"That same van showed up on security footage taken outside your condo," she said.

"So the driver must have planted the bomb," he mused. He wasn't surprised, though. The guy was obviously a pro. "Any way of figuring out who it's registered to?"

"A rental company for commercial vehicles," she said. "The company that leased it from them doesn't exist. The paperwork was fake."

He cursed, and Wendy turned toward him. "So the bomber is definitely a professional," he said.

"I'd say so," Nikki said with a heavy sigh that rattled his cell phone. "Especially since he must have followed one of us here. That van is parked in the hotel lot."

He cursed again, more vehemently this time. "Can you take him?"

Preferably before he got anywhere near their hotel room and Wendy.

"The van is empty," Nikki conceded. "He got away from us."

Hart clicked the mute button on his phone and told Wendy, "Get dressed. We have to get out of here."

Then he clicked off the mute and told Nikki, "The bastard could be setting a bomb somewhere in the hotel if he hasn't already."

It certainly hadn't taken him long to set the one on his Payne Protection SUV.

"I know," Nikki agreed. "Wait until we can get more backup—"

But Hart had already clicked off the cell. He couldn't wait, not with the possibility that a bomb could detonate at any time. "We have to get the hell out of here," he said.

Wendy nodded in agreement.

"It could be a trap," he warned her. "Just a way to flush us out of the hotel."

Why else would the bomber have driven the van here that had nearly run them off the road? He must have wanted him or another bodyguard to see it and to know that he was near.

He was a sick bastard, so it was no wonder that he worked for Luther Mills.

"You have to stop calling me," came the protest, the voice rising with panic.

Luther smiled in enjoyment of the fear. That was how it was damn well supposed to be.

People were supposed to be scared of him. Too scared to cross him…

And damn well too scared to testify against him.

But neither little Rosie Mendez nor that CSI Wendy Thompson had backed down. They weren't afraid of him yet. But they should be.

They would be.

"This is an untraceable cell," Luther said assuredly. "Nobody will figure out that you're working for me."

Actually, they would once the evidence disappeared. But by then it would be too late.

Chapter 17

Fear gripped Wendy. She remembered the sound of the blast when Hart's agency SUV had exploded. It was a miracle no one had been injured. But if an explosion went off in a hotel that was fully booked...

She shuddered to think of the number of possible casualties. "We need to evacuate the hotel," she murmured to Hart as they exited their room. Or innocent people might die because of her.

Fortunately, the hallway was empty but for the two of them. Nobody would be caught in the cross fire in this corridor. But the bomber couldn't know which floor they were on; Hart hadn't registered under his name or hers.

"Backup is already in the parking lot," Hart said. "They'll take care of it. My job is to take care of you."

He certainly had just a short time ago—when he'd made love to her. But it hadn't been love. It had just been sex. She'd said it herself and she knew that was the only reason he'd touched her again.

She'd seen his concern earlier, his fear and guilt that she might be falling for him. That her crush had become serious. It had, but that was her fault, not his. Wasn't it typical for a woman to fall for the man who kept saving her life?

It had to be some kind of occupational hazard of being a bodyguard. Kind of like getting blown up or shot at...

They had just stepped into the stairwell when the shots rang out, pinging off the concrete walls. Hart covered her body with his as he drew his weapon. Then he pointed his gun down the stairwell and fired back.

After the shots stopped reverberating, footsteps echoed throughout the stairwell as the shooter ran away. An outside door opened, an alarm sounding.

"Go after him," Wendy said.

"Are you okay?" he asked.

She nodded. "I'm fine."

When Hart started down the stairwell in pursuit, she saw the blood. It wasn't hers. Hart had been hit.

She ran after him, calling out, "You're bleeding."

Whatever his injury, he moved quickly, until he got to the door at the bottom. Then he paused and she caught up with him.

Blood oozed from a deep scratch on his cheek. Either a bullet or a piece of the concrete block that the bullets had chipped had struck him. She reached out. But before her fingers could touch his wound, he pulled back.

Then he turned his focus on that steel door, staring at it like he hoped he could stare through it.

"It could be a trap," he said.

She shook her head. "He had no time to set any explosive devices outside. He would have blown himself up with the way he ran out of here."

She suspected he might have been hit, as well. The farther she'd descended the stairs, the more blood she'd seen. Droplets turning into small pools. Hart hadn't been injured badly enough to bleed that much, so at least one of Hart's bullets must have struck him.

But being injured didn't make him any less dangerous. In fact, she had once found a dog at a crime scene that'd been shot, and when she'd tried to help it, it had, out of fear and desperation, attacked her. She had a scar on her forearm where his teeth had torn her skin.

"Open that door slowly," she advised Hart.

"You said it shouldn't be rigged," he reminded her, his brown eyes narrowed in skepticism.

"Not with explosives," she said. "But that doesn't mean he's not waiting to shoot your head off the moment you step outside."

Hart nodded then pushed her firmly behind him as he pulled open the door. He ducked low, so if the bomber shot at him, the bullet would whiz over his head.

Predictably, one did, striking the concrete wall behind them. Thankfully it didn't ricochet, just chipped the cement, raising a cloud of dust inside the stairwell.

"I don't like this," Hart murmured.

"Of course not," Wendy agreed. "Who the hell enjoys getting shot at?"

"He's holding us in here," he said. "He might have set a bomb inside the stairwell, sometime before Nikki had noticed the van in the lot."

Wendy glanced up. He was right. It was a possibility. If the guy had set it on a higher floor, the whole thing could collapse on them.

Hart must have realized the same thing because there was a sense of urgency in his deep voice when he said, "We need to get out of here."

She nodded.

"On my count, we both start firing our weapons," he said, his palm pressed flat against the steel exit door.

She nodded again even as she swallowed hard. Since she didn't want to accidentally shoot an innocent person, she would just aim high.

But when Hart pushed open the door, he kept his body between hers and the outside, not even giving her a chance to fire her weapon.

He barely got a chance to fire his weapon before he fell onto the sidewalk leading to the parking lot. He had been hit this time, and it wasn't with just a chip of concrete. He'd been hit with a bullet.

"Hart!" she screamed as she followed him out. Standing protectively over him, she raised her weapon to fire it, but no more shots rang out. She was safe, but her bodyguard was down.

"Hart! Hart!" She dropped to her knees beside him and silently prayed that he would be all right.

* * *

Hart cursed as he pushed himself up from the sidewalk and pain radiated through his leg. It shook and threatened to fold beneath him as blood ran down to pool in his boot.

"Sit down," Wendy said. "You're making it bleed more."

Hart didn't give a damn about his leg right now. The bullet must have just grazed the fleshy part of his thigh. While he was bleeding, the blood wasn't gushing out of the wound, so no artery had been hit.

What about Wendy?

"Are you all right?" he asked as he glanced around. Where the hell had the shooter gone?

Other Payne Protection bodyguards ran up now, guns drawn. Maybe they had scared him off.

"You were supposed to wait for backup to come to your room," Nikki admonished him.

"And get blown up in the hotel?" He reached for Wendy, grasping her arm to lead her farther from the structure in case it exploded like his SUV had. But he had to lean heavily against her and he wondered who was leading whom.

"River City PD bomb unit is coming out," Nikki assured him. And the parking lot was filling with guests, so an evacuation must have begun.

"We have to get him to the hospital," Wendy said. "He could bleed out."

"I'm fine," Hart insisted, but he had to say it through teeth gritted in agony. His thigh burned, the pain radiating from the wound.

"You need medical attention," she insisted. Then she

ignored him and turned to Nikki and Lars. "Can you get a vehicle?"

Nikki nodded at her husband, who turned and ran toward the parking lot. His long legs ate up the distance and within seconds an SUV squealed to a stop at the end of the sidewalk.

Wendy had become more Hart's crutch than his assignment as she led him to the vehicle.

Nikki rushed forward and pulled open the back door. "Stay low," she told Wendy. "We don't know that he's out of the area yet." Then she spoke to her husband through the open driver's window. "Make sure you aren't followed."

Lars chuckled. "Who? Me? Not going to happen…"

But the shooter had followed someone to the hotel. Hart had carefully watched his rearview, so he didn't think he was the one who'd been followed. Since he hadn't noticed the white van a couple of other times until it was too late, he couldn't swear it hadn't been his fault, though.

"Get in," Wendy urged him.

As she helped him into the back seat, Hart grunted with pain. But before he could give in to the stream of curses burning in his throat, his cell began to ring. It was probably Parker, going to blast him like Nikki had for not waiting for backup. But when he pulled it from his pocket, the screen showed Unknown Caller.

A sick feeling in his stomach, he clicked to accept and asked, "Who is this?"

"Daddy?" a familiar soft voice asked, wobbling with emotion.

His sharp tone had probably frightened her. He deliberately lowered it. "Is this my best girl?"

She giggled and replied, "Yes." Then she paused for a moment before asking, "Or is Winnie your best girl?"

"Winnie is…" He glanced over at her. Her red hair was tangled around her face, which was pale with fear. For him…

She hadn't been that frightened for herself. The way she'd followed him out of the hotel…

She could have been shot. He was actually damn surprised that she hadn't been. And damn glad…

"Winnie is a woman," he said. A strong woman.

And a passionate one. But he wouldn't allow himself to think about what had happened in that hotel room before Nikki's call. He wouldn't allow himself to dwell on how he'd crossed that line again with Wendy even though he'd promised himself that he wouldn't.

But he hadn't been able to resist her.

She leaned forward and whispered to Lars to hurry to the hospital. The SUV lurched forward as Lars pressed hard on the accelerator and the vehicle squealed off.

Hart flinched as the sudden movement jarred his wound, but he held back a grunt. Then he assured his daughter, "You're my best girl."

"You sound funny, Daddy," his daughter remarked.

She knew him well. For so long they had been all each other had had. But now there were the Thompsons.

He changed his voice into an imitation of one of her favorite cartoon characters and replied, "I am a funny guy."

She giggled.

Then he asked, "Are you having fun, honey?"

She proceeded to tell him about all the fun they were having—the games they'd played, the cookies they'd baked—and his heart began to throb and ache more than his wounded leg. She hadn't been gone very long at all, but he already missed her so damn much.

Lars must have driven fast because they were at the hospital before Felicity had finished talking to him. Wendy reached for the door handle, but he grabbed her hand and stopped her.

The shooter might have followed them. Or he might have beaten them to the hospital and was waiting for another try at taking out Wendy.

"Hey, baby," he said into the phone. "I have to go now, but I will talk to you soon. I love you, honey."

"Love you, too, Daddy."

He had to brace himself to click the disconnect button. He hated to let her go, hated that he had to be away from her right now.

But she loved Winnie and wouldn't want anything to happen to her. And he felt the same…about not wanting anything to happen to her.

Felicity was the only female he would ever trust enough to give his heart.

The bad feeling that had gripped Parker for days had eased somewhat when the hotel had been found to have no explosives inside it. But Hart had still been hurt. And Parker rushed through the sliding doors of the hospital, anxious to find out how he was doing.

Lars was always easy to spot given the way he towered head and shoulders over everyone else in the waiting room. He stood next to a smaller woman, not Nikki, though. This woman's curls were bright red, not Nikki's auburn. And Parker's sister had never looked at him the way that Wendy Thompson did as he approached. His steps slowed somewhat as he saw the anger burning in her green eyes.

"How is he?" Parker asked. Was the injury more severe than the through-and-through Nikki had assured him it was?

"Not very damn good, thanks to you!" Wendy said, her voice sharp with the fury he could see in her eyes.

Lars shook his head. "He's going to be fine. He's getting some stitches and a pair of crutches. He should be out soon."

"And when he comes out here, you need to fire him," Wendy persisted.

Parker narrowed his eyes. "For what?" As far as he could see, she was unscathed. "You're not hurt. He saved your life. He's doing his job."

Damn well. All the members of Parker's carefully chosen team had proved to be excellent bodyguards.

"Doing his job is going to get him killed," Wendy said, and now her voice cracked. And tears rushed in to join the anger in her eyes.

"It's the risk we all take," Lars told her, his deep voice soft with sympathy.

"But he has a child," Wendy said. "And he is all that child has."

Parker flinched. She was right. He knew it.

"He's a great bodyguard," Wendy said. "But this assignment…"

Her.

"It's just too dangerous," she continued. "Luther Mills is too dangerous."

"That's why you need a bodyguard," Parker argued.

She nodded in agreement. "A bodyguard, yes. But not Hart. Anyone but Hart. The next time the bullet might not go through him without hitting anything vital. The next bullet or explosion could kill him. That's a risk that I'm not willing to take."

For his daughter's sake? Or for hers?

It was obvious that Wendy Thompson cared about Hart. Then, of course, even Parker had heard the rumors about her crush on Detective Fisher. That crush had apparently become something more. Just for her or for Hart, too?

Hart might not appreciate what Parker was going to do, but he had to acknowledge that she was right. Hart could no longer be her bodyguard.

Chapter 18

Hart's throat burned from all the shouting he'd done. Not because he was in pain, although his damn leg continued to throb. Maybe he shouldn't have refused the painkillers. But he hadn't wanted any drugs to affect his ability to carry out his assignment.

"You can't just take my job away," he protested.

Parker, in the driver's seat, glanced over the console at him. "You still have a job," he assured him. "I'm not firing you."

"You fired me from this assignment!"

Parker uttered a weary-sounding sigh. He was probably tired of arguing with him. Not that he'd argued much. He'd just reminded Hart that he was the boss and this was the way it was going to be.

"You're injured," Parker said.

He snorted. "Like you and every other Payne Protection bodyguard hasn't got hurt and still continued to do his or her job." He'd heard the stories—the legends—about his boss and coworkers.

"You have a child," Parker said, as if Hart needed reminding.

"And you don't?"

"I don't put myself in danger the way you are right now," Parker pointed out.

"Taking this job for the chief—that puts you in danger, too!" Hart quipped. "You don't think Luther Mills wouldn't love to take out every damn one of us?" He had probably put out a hit on every one of them as well as the people involved in prosecuting him.

"He's not going to have the chance to take you out," Parker said. "You're going to go be with your daughter. You can help protect the Thompsons."

Hart shook his head. "No."

"You don't want to be with Felicity?"

"Of course I do," he said. "But I don't want to leave Wendy alone and unprotected." He'd promised her father that he would protect Ben Thompson's daughter like Ben Thompson had promised to protect his. Hart would not break that promise.

Parker glanced at him again, his eyes narrowed. "You think I would leave her alone and unprotected? Of course I assigned someone else to protect her."

"Lars?" he asked. They'd both been gone when he'd hobbled out on his crutches to the waiting room. His heart had plummeted in his chest when she hadn't been there. "I can't believe she went along with you removing me as bodyguard."

Parker's voice was low and quiet when he replied, "It was her idea."

Hart jumped as if his boss had shouted. It was her idea.

She didn't want him any longer.

"You're injured," Parker repeated. "You need to either take some time off or to take an easier assignment, like protecting the Thompsons."

Hart shook his head. He didn't believe they were in danger any longer. Luther wasn't trying to threaten and intimidate Wendy anymore. He was outright trying to kill her. He wanted her gone.

"Where is she?" he asked.

Parker sighed. "What does it matter?" he asked. "You're not going there."

"Work," he said. "She must be at work…" He shook his head. "It's too dangerous. No civilian is allowed to go into the police lab." He hadn't been able to go inside with her; he'd had to stand guard in the hallway.

"Nothing happened to her when you were outside the lab," Parker reminded him. "Nobody's going to try anything inside the police department."

Hart was not so sure. He had this sick feeling in his stomach. "I don't know…" He shook his head. "Luther's getting desperate enough to try anything."

And being desperate made Luther Mills more dangerous than he had ever been.

"She'll be fine," Parker assured him. "Nothing will happen to her."

His promise rang hollow. They both knew that he had no way of guaranteeing her safety.

Luther had someone on the inside of the River City PD. Or maybe even several someones. That meant it wasn't just possible that one of them would get to Wendy; it was probable.

Unlike Parker's, Hart's promise to her father had not been hollow. He fully intended to keep it. It didn't matter that Parker had removed him from the assignment. Hell, it wouldn't matter if he fired him.

He was going to protect Wendy Thompson, even if he died trying.

Woodrow was frustrated as hell. He'd spent weeks trying to figure out who the leak was within his precinct. It couldn't have been just that rookie cop who had tried to kill the eyewitness.

There had to be someone higher. Someone with more inside information. The district attorney's office was working on finding their leak. But with the district attorney on maternity leave, Woodrow had to trust that her subordinates would be able to handle the investigation.

Hell, they couldn't be doing any worse than he was. He needed to find his. So he'd called in a reinforcement.

Woodrow's stepson and former FBI colleague sat across from him, across the desk from the one he used to sit behind as the former acting chief of the River City Police Department. Hell, Woodrow had been the one who'd recommended his best FBI agent for the job of cleaning up the corruption in River City.

At that time Nick had been using Rus as his last name. He hadn't changed it to Payne until his family had accepted the illegitimate child of Nicholas Payne Senior. With black hair and bright blue eyes, he looked just like his late father and his brothers. Woodrow's bride, Penny, had been the first to accept him, of course. Her heart was so big, but in Nick she had also found a kindred spirit. The guy, like her, was legendary for his uncanny ability to just *know* things.

"So what do you know?" Woodrow asked him.

Nick shook his head. "I know Luther Mills is a very dangerous man, and my one regret was that I was not able to personally take him down before my job as acting chief ended."

Nick could have become the full-time chief but had turned down the offer to join the family business and become a bodyguard instead. He was one of Logan Payne's team now, but Woodrow suspected he would soon be starting his own branch of the Payne Protection Agency. His team would probably consist of former FBI agents.

So Woodrow was happy he'd given up his former job as Bureau chief. He probably would have eventually lost all his good agents to Nick.

"I want to make sure Mills goes down," Woodrow said. "But I need your help to do that."

"You hired Parker's team," Nick reminded him.

Woodrow nodded. "The former vice cops know Luther best." They were well aware of the dangers of taking on the notorious drug dealer since they'd all done it before.

Nick nodded. "Yes. So why am I here?"

"You know this station house better than anyone," Woodrow said. "I need to know which one of these officers is Luther's informant."

Nick's broad shoulders sagged slightly as if they still carried a heavy burden. "I tried my best," he said. "But I couldn't find all the corrupt officers. And even some of the ones I found, the ones I suspected, I didn't have enough to prove those suspicions."

Woodrow already knew that. "I want to talk about those suspicions," he said. "Who sticks out to you?"

Nick shrugged. "Really, most of the ones about whom I had suspicions either quit or took early retirement once the witch hunt—as they called it—started. I don't know who you have left." He turned and looked through the window at the detectives' bull pen.

Woodrow wasn't certain that was where his leak was, though. He hated to think a detective was on Luther Mills's payroll. "What about the evidence techs?" he asked. "Anybody come to mind?"

"Not Wendy Thompson," Nick assured him. "She was the best, even when she first started. Brilliant mind and total recall. She's an unshakable witness, too. I totally understand why Luther's so determined to take her out. I hope she's someplace safe."

She was in the building. The chief had been alerted when she'd passed through the security checkpoint to enter the lobby. Ordinarily he would think there was no place safer than the police department, but until he knew who the leak was, it was probably more dangerous than anywhere else she could be.

She could be anywhere else. But he knew why she was there. To see if the evidence from the bomb planted on Hart Fisher's Payne Protection Agency SUV had been processed yet.

"Well, we both know it's not Wendy," Woodrow said then prodded Nick, "Anyone you can think of?"

The younger man tilted his head as if searching his memory. He nodded. "Older guy. Terrance Gibbs. He had a kid who was caught dealing for Luther. But, like the others, he took early retirement before I could find anything to prove he might have been working with him."

The chief tensed. "The supervisor for the lab…she said she just approved a request for a tech to return on a part-time basis. He wanted to supplement his retirement…"

"Gibbs?" Nick asked.

He nodded grimly.

"It's not the River City PD that's going to supplement that retirement," Nick warned him. "It's Luther Mills."

Woodrow already had the phone in his hand. He wanted to know where the hell Gibbs was right now. He hoped nowhere near Wendy Thompson.

Wendy had thought the tight feeling in her chest would ease once Hart was no longer her bodyguard. She'd thought she would feel better once he was out of danger and hopefully on his way to reuniting with his sweet daughter. She'd seen the pain on his face during his phone call with Felicity; that pain hadn't been entirely because of the gunshot wound to his leg. It had been clear how much he missed his child and that he ached to be with her again.

Like Wendy ached to be with him.

But this was for the best. She'd done the right thing when she'd convinced his boss to take him off her assignment. It was too dangerous for a single father. Too dangerous for her. The more time she'd spent with Hart, the more she'd fallen for him—even before they'd made love.

At least, she'd made love. To him, it had just been sex. And that was why this was better for her, too. He was never going to return her feelings, so it was best that she kept her distance before she got hurt even more than she was hurting now. She drew in a deep breath, inhaling all the familiar scents of the lab. This was where she belonged, processing evidence, putting away more criminals like Luther Mills.

As she breathed deep, she smelled something unfamiliar to the lab. It was a chemical, but one of a commercial fragrance. A man's cologne. She didn't know anyone who wore that particular scent anymore.

It was the cologne of an older generation. Her father used to use it before she and her mother had staged an intervention and found him a better-smelling fragrance. All the current evidence techs were pretty young, except her supervisor. But Sandy didn't wear any perfume, let alone a man's cologne.

Wendy had also thought she would be alone in the lab since it was so late. But then she saw the gray-haired man standing over a computer, tapping on the keyboard. He glanced up at her and his dark eyes narrowed.

Wendy's blood chilled. "Terrance," she murmured. "I thought you retired…"

"I came back to help out," he said as he tried to

curve his lips into a smile. It was tight and didn't reach his eyes.

In that moment she knew he hadn't come back to help out her or the River City PD. She reached for her weapon. But before she could pull it from her bag, he already had a gun barrel pointing at her.

"Where is it?" he asked.

"What are you doing, Terrance?" she asked him.

He closed his eyes and sucked in a deep breath, as if bracing himself. When he did, she eased back a step toward the door. "Don't move," he said. "Don't make me pull this trigger…"

"If you do, it'll all be over," she warned him. "My bodyguard is right outside the door."

Lars hadn't wanted to stay out there. But she hadn't wanted the presence of a civilian to affect the chain of evidence.

Terrance tapped the end of the gun barrel. "Silencer. He won't hear a thing."

"I can scream," she said. She knew that she already should have. However, she wasn't convinced Terrance would actually pull that trigger. It was one thing to tamper with evidence; it was another to murder.

"And I'll kill you," he said. He shook his head as if he pitied her. "Why didn't you just listen to the warnings? Why didn't you destroy that damn evidence yourself?"

"Because Javier Mendez deserves justice."

"Javier Mendez?" he asked.

"The kid Luther murdered." Terrance didn't even know his name. Maybe he'd made it a point not to know, so it wouldn't bother him to help Luther. "Mills needs to be brought to justice for his crimes."

"Justice?" Terrance grunted derisively. "You are so young and naive."

Hart had once told her the same thing. So had the chief. It had been true—until now.

"Were you behind those warnings?" she asked.

"Luther didn't call me in until after you failed to heed his warnings," he replied.

Her pulse quickened with excitement. Here was the key. This man was the proof that Luther was threatening prosecution witnesses. She wished she could reach inside her bag, not for the gun but for her phone. So she could press the record button.

Terrance stepped forward and jerked the bag from her hand. He was not naive; he didn't trust her at all.

"So you set the bomb?" she asked.

His brow furrowed with confusion. "Bomb? There was no bomb on that car. I cut the brake line. I thought you might get the message then. But, nope, you refused to destroy that evidence."

He glanced inside her purse as if it were large enough to contain everything she'd collected from Javier Mendez's crime scene. Luther had been sloppy; he'd left a lot behind for her to find. But maybe he hadn't been careless so much as confident that whatever evidence he'd left would disappear as it had all the times before.

Gibbs probably didn't realize how much she'd collected or maybe he was looking for a key for a safe-deposit box or something because he upended her purse onto the stainless-steel countertop. Her gun clanked, metal against metal, as it dropped.

Her fingers twitched. She wanted to reach for it. Or for her cell. But he picked up her cell and tossed it to the floor, where it broke.

She flinched.

"You didn't put it in the evidence room," he said.

Of course she hadn't. She wouldn't have been able to control who had access to it then. And she wasn't quite as naive as everyone had thought she was.

"So where is it?" he asked.

"It's been turned over to the district attorney's office," she lied.

He laughed. "Luther would know if that was the case. They don't have it yet."

Apparently it was a good thing that they didn't or it would have likely already been destroyed. She shivered as a chill rushed over her.

"I talked to other people in the lab," he continued. "It sounds like you're the only one who knows where it is." He stepped closer and pressed the gun barrel to her head. "So it sounds like if you're dead, the evidence will be, too. Nobody will find it."

He cocked the gun.

She swallowed hard. "If something happens to me, the evidence will turn up," she said. And she wasn't bluffing right now.

When the threats had come in, she'd put a plan in place in case Luther made good on those threats. "Rest assured that Jocelyn Gerber will receive everything she needs to put Luther Mills away for the rest of his miserable life."

Terrance studied her, as if debating whether she was lying again, like she had about the district attorney having the evidence, or if she was telling the truth.

She returned his stare without even blinking.

He shook his head, rejecting the truth. "You're too trusting. You probably didn't think it would actually come to this."

"To what?" she asked.

"To your death."

Chapter 19

Hart's chest ached as panic pressed hard on his lungs. He ditched his crutches and ran down the basement hallway toward the evidence lab. The chief had called him, thinking that he was still Wendy's bodyguard, as he should have been. He'd warned Hart about the return of the retired evidence tech. Fortunately, Hart had already insisted that Parker drop him off at the police station, so he'd been inside when he'd taken the chief's call. He'd had only to wait until the damn elevator doors had opened to the basement.

As he neared the door to the lab, a hulking shadow stepped away from the wall and metal glinted in the fluorescent light buzzing overhead. "What's the rush?" Lars asked as he lowered his weapon.

"Is she in there?" Hart asked.

Lars nodded.

"Is she alone?"

Lars shrugged. "She wouldn't let me inside, so I couldn't check. She told me that it should be empty since it was so late."

But it wasn't. Hart just knew—from the chill that passed through him—that she was not alone.

That she was in danger.

"What is it?" Lars asked as if he sensed it, too. "What's going on?"

Hart shook his head. He didn't want to risk the guy overhearing their conversation. So he just whispered, "Is there another way in?"

Lars shrugged.

"Find out," Hart implored him. "Then you go in that way…"

"What are you doing?" Lars asked. "You're not even supposed to be working this assignment anymore."

Hart cursed, letting the ex-Marine know what he thought about that. He didn't give a damn who was supposed to be protecting Wendy now. He'd promised he would, and that wasn't a promise he was about to break. That was why he'd convinced Parker to drop him here.

Lars shrugged again and headed off down the hall, looking for that other entrance.

Hart took a deep breath as he drew his gun and pushed open the door to the lab. Fortunately, Wendy hadn't locked it, as she had every time he'd been standing in the hallway outside the lab. She must not have trusted him to stay out like she'd trusted Lars.

"Get out!" someone shouted at him.

It wasn't Wendy. She said nothing, just glanced over her shoulder to see who'd entered. He saw the emotions pass through her eyes. The initial one had been fear, then a flicker of relief, only to be replaced again with fear.

Duck.

He silently shouted the order, hoping she would see it in his eyes. But she turned back to the man holding the gun to her head.

"If I leave, I'm sending in a whole barrage of officers to take you out," Hart warned the man.

The guy moved his gun from Wendy to gesture at Hart. "Then come on in," he urged. "You can die with this stubborn bitch."

"No!" Wendy said. "Hart, get out of here!"

"Hart Fisher," the man remarked. "I didn't think you were with the River City PD anymore."

Hart recognized the retired evidence tech then. "I didn't think you were, either, Terrance. What brings you back?" He could guess. Luther Mills.

Terrance's head bobbed. "That's right," he said as if he'd just remembered. "You're working for Parker Payne. You're her bodyguard."

"No!" Wendy protested. "Not anymore. Not since you shot him at the hotel."

Terrance Gibbs's brow furrowed with even more wrinkles. "What? What hotel?" He shook his head. "It doesn't matter. Nothing matters but getting rid of that evidence."

"I'll never give it to you," Wendy vowed.

Hart believed her. She wouldn't do it—even to save her own life.

The retired tech must have realized it, as well, because he turned back toward her. But he pointed his gun at Hart. "What if I shoot him?" he asked. "Will you tell me then?"

Her throat moved as she swallowed hard. She shook her head.

The guy appeared ready to call her bluff. But before he could squeeze the trigger, she grabbed his arm, struggling to knock the gun from his grasp.

Hart took his shot.

His bullet dropped Terrance Gibbs to the floor. And Wendy dropped with him.

"Are you all right?" he asked as he limped forward, rushing to her side.

She knelt beside Terrance, checking for a pulse even as blood pooled beneath his head. "No!" she said. "Damn you! No! Why the hell did you do that?"

"Save your life?" He shook his head. "I don't know. Because it's my job?"

She shook hers. "Not anymore. You're not my bodyguard, Hart. You shouldn't be here."

"And you'd be dead if I wasn't."

"It's true," a deep voice murmured as Lars entered the lab behind him. "I didn't realize you weren't alone."

"I wasn't alone, but I wasn't in danger," Wendy replied.

Hart pointed at the gun still grasped tightly in the hand of the dead evidence tech. "He was going to shoot you."

She shook her head. "No, he was going to shoot you. He could have shot me any time before you came in, but he couldn't bring himself to do it. He's not a killer."

Lisa Childs   217

"My SUV might say something different. He sure murdered that."

"He didn't set the bomb," she said.

Hart shook his head. "It doesn't matter what he did or some other lackey of Luther's did. He was still going to shoot you."

That pain in his chest returned, squeezing his heart tightly as he considered what might have happened had he been just a few minutes later, had he found her dead...

He couldn't imagine a world without Wendy Thompson in it. He didn't want to. He'd thought that because he couldn't trust a woman again, he wouldn't be able to love one. He'd been wrong.

Despite his best efforts to fight his feelings, he'd fallen for Wendy.

Hart fell silent as more officers rushed into the lab.

Even the chief joined them as well as Nick Payne. "Are you okay?" Lynch asked Wendy, his deep voice full of concern.

She nodded.

"And the evidence?" he asked almost reluctantly, as if it were a sore subject.

Wendy nodded again. "It's safe."

The chief squeezed her shoulder. "Good work."

"Hart shot him," she said. "I think we could have turned him against Luther." She glanced down at the dead man as if there was still some hope he might talk.

But it wouldn't have mattered had he lived; Hart doubted the guy would have ever rolled on Luther Mills.

And if he had, he would have wound up just as dead as he was now.

"We don't need him," the chief said. "Not as long as we have you and the evidence." He looked back to Hart. "We don't know who else might be working with Mills. We need to get her out of here, get her someplace safe."

Hart shook his head. "I'm not her bodyguard anymore." He pointed to Lars. "He is…" Then he turned and hobbled toward the door.

He wasn't the man to protect her. He was the man who needed protection from her. He'd lost his heart to her and, because of that, because he was distracted, he might lose his life and hers if he continued to try to protect her.

No. He trusted that the chief and Parker would make sure she didn't have a call as close as this one again. He wasn't so arrogant to think that he was the best bodyguard. There were men and women who'd been doing it longer and better than he had.

No. It was safer—for both of them—if someone other than he was Wendy's bodyguard.

What had she done? What had she said? What had caused Hart to suddenly walk away from the assignment as if he'd been anxious to go? To leave her?

Sure, Wendy hadn't been very gracious or grateful that he'd saved her life. And she had to admit to herself now that he had. She wanted to believe that Terrance Gibbs wouldn't have pulled the trigger. But he'd been desperate.

The day after the shooting in the lab, she'd learned

from the chief's investigation that Gibbs's son had been in debt to Luther. His kid would have died had Terrance not done as Luther ordered.

Since it was between Wendy's life or his son's, she had no doubt that Gibbs would have chosen his son's. Hart had been right to shoot him.

To save her as he had so many times before. But then he'd just walked, or rather, he'd limped off. Maybe he'd been in too much pain from his gunshot wound. She'd seen the grimace on his face as he'd crossed the lab.

Or maybe he'd just been missing his daughter too much to stay away from Felicity any longer. Like Terrance Gibbs, Hart would choose his child every time.

That was the way it should be. Wendy wasn't jealous of Felicity. She knew it didn't matter whether Hart had a child or not. Even if he wasn't a father, he wouldn't have fallen for Wendy.

She had been nothing but an assignment to him. And, until that assignment, he hadn't ever paid her any attention despite her crush on him.

Heat rushed to her face. Then she remembered those times they'd made love and heat rushed to other parts of her body.

Hart had warned her not to have any expectations, that he would never marry again. Was he not entirely over his ex-wife? Was that why he couldn't give his heart to anyone else? Or was it that she'd hurt him so badly that he would never trust another woman?

"You okay?" Nikki Payne-Ecklund asked her.

Wendy sighed and then nodded. Nikki was a good

bodyguard; she'd proved herself to her brothers and to Wendy herself.

Yet Wendy didn't feel quite as safe as she had when Hart had been protecting her. The only thing he had failed to protect was her heart, despite his efforts to warn her against falling for him.

When he'd walked away, he'd broken it—her heart. She doubted she would recover any more than he had after his divorce.

"It's just hard…" Wendy murmured. "Not working."

Nikki smiled. "It's just been a day."

"But there's evidence to process. The bomb fragments…" Frustration nagged at her, not just that she couldn't work, but about those crime scenes, the ones at the SUV explosion and the hotel…

Something wasn't right.

"I don't think it's just work you're missing," Nikki said with a smile.

"This isn't about Hart," Wendy protested. But it was a lie. It was about Hart. Everything was about Hart for her. "He needs to be with his daughter."

Nikki bobbed her head in agreement.

"Is he?" she asked hopefully.

Nikki shrugged. "I don't know. The chief and Parker are keeping her and your parents' whereabouts top secret. They don't want anyone to find them."

"Not even Hart?"

"They're both parents," Nikki said. "I'm sure they will tell him. But no one else can know."

Wendy got the message. She wouldn't be able to see

her parents or Felicity. That was good. Being close to her had only put them in danger, like it had Hart.

He was much safer away from her. But that ache in her chest didn't ease. Maybe she just ached for missing him, though, because she did miss him. So damn much…

And it had only been a day.

Luther cursed. He'd been warned the day before that Gibbs was dead. And the son of a bitch had run his mouth off before he died.

But his lawyer had assured him it didn't matter. Since he was dead, he couldn't testify against him. And anything he might have said to Wendy Thompson or Hart Fisher was inadmissible in court since it was all just hearsay.

No. Hart had done him a favor when he'd killed the evidence tech. But Gibbs wasn't the tech that Luther really wanted dead. He had to get rid of Wendy Thompson once and for all—before she disappeared like her parents had, like the eyewitness had. And he had no doubt that she eventually would.

The Payne Protection Agency was too damn good. So good that Luther probably needed to get rid of every damn one of them. And he knew just where he would start. With Hart Fisher.

Chapter 20

"Someone wants to talk to you," Nikki said as she held out her cell phone to Wendy.

Her hand shook as she took it. Was it Hart? Had he realized that he cared about her, too? God, she was still being too naive if she seriously expected that to happen.

She had only been an assignment to him. One that, after his initial anger over being removed, he'd had no problem walking away from…

"Hello," she said slowly, cautiously.

"Winnie!" a young voice squealed, and the cell speaker rattled.

Wendy smiled. "Hey, my beautiful princess, how are you doing?"

"Good," Hart's daughter replied. "Me and Mama

Mags made the cookies you made with her when you was little like me."

Mama Mags. That was what her father had always had his football team call his wife. She'd claimed she hated it, but she'd smiled every time one of them had used it. That was what Wendy wanted someday for herself: the same kind of relationship her parents had. One that was full of love and teasing and trust.

She would never have that with Hart. He'd been broken when his ex-wife had shattered his heart. He wouldn't be able to trust again.

Wendy could hardly blame him. Her heart ached so much that she knew she wouldn't willingly risk it again.

"You'll have to save some of those cookies for me," Wendy told the little girl. "They're my favorite." She had no idea what kind they'd made, though. Her mother loved to bake and Wendy had had many favorites.

"Daddy's coming," Felicity said. "But I won't let him eat all of them."

"Okay," Wendy said, her voice cracking a little with emotion. She wanted to be there, too.

As if she had the same longing, Felicity asked, "When are you coming?"

"I…I still have work to do," Wendy replied. And she did—if anyone would let her back into her damn lab. Of course, it, too, had become a crime scene.

For a crime against her, so she wouldn't be able to process it just as she hadn't been able to process the others.

She had never thanked Hart for once again saving

her life. She had a sick feeling in the pit of her stomach that she might never have the chance.

"When is your daddy supposed to get there?" she asked Felicity.

The little girl's voice was muffled as she repeated the question to someone else. Then another voice replaced Felicity's high-pitched one.

"Hello, sweetheart," Mom greeted Wendy. "How are you doing?"

Not well. But she wouldn't admit that to her mother. "Good," she said.

Her mother sighed. "You're not good at that, Wendy."

Lying.

She knew. They'd caught her in every single lie she'd ever told them.

"I am still worried about all of you," Wendy admitted. "Are you really doing fine?"

"Yes," her mother said. "We are having so much fun with this amazing little princess. You need to join us, sweetheart. Then everything would be perfect."

Tears stung her eyes as Wendy imagined how that could be. Her parents, that sweet little girl and Hart, all together, laughing, cooking, enjoying each other's company.

But that would never happen. Because Wendy was in danger. And Hart didn't love her.

She blinked back the rush of tears and wrinkled her nose against the sting of them. "No," Wendy replied. "I can't join you. I would only put you all in danger."

"Wendy—"

She ignored her mom's interruption and continued. "Like I did Hart."

"Is that why he's coming here without you? Did you fire him?"

She hadn't been able to do that; she wouldn't have wanted to. He really was an amazing bodyguard. She wouldn't have survived this long without him.

"I convinced his boss to reassign him," she explained. "To a less dangerous assignment."

"Wendy—"

"He's a single father, Mom," she reminded her. "I wouldn't be able to live with myself if Felicity lost her daddy because of me."

"Luther Mills," her mother corrected her. "He's responsible for all of this. Not you."

That was true. But if she was like the others—like Terrance Gibbs and that rookie cop and all the ones who'd helped Luther cover up his crimes—she wouldn't be in danger and neither would anyone she cared about.

Then again, Gibbs and the rookie were dead.

Maybe, eventually, people would figure out that they had more to fear from working for Luther than against him. She only hoped that happened before anyone else got hurt.

She flinched as she remembered how Hart had fallen when that bullet had taken him down. For one horrific moment she'd thought he was dead. That Felicity's father was gone.

Wendy's lover...

But he wasn't her lover. He didn't love her. But she loved him—enough to let him go to keep him safe.

What if he wasn't in danger only because of her?

The thought had been niggling at her for a while now. Because of that bomb and the shooting at the hotel.

They didn't make sense to her.

"Do you know when Hart was supposed to be there?" she asked.

She could hear the smile in her mother's voice when she replied, "Were you hoping to speak to him, too?"

No. She would be embarrassed for him to think that she'd had Nikki call so she could talk to him. He would probably think she was stalking him.

"I just wondered if he was late."

Her mother paused for a long moment. "Now that you mention it, we did think he was arriving this morning."

It was afternoon.

"Okay, Mom, I need to go now," Wendy said. She needed to find Hart. Not to speak to him but just to make sure that he was okay. "I'll talk to you soon. And I'll see you when the trial is over."

"Oh, Wendy, are you sure you have to wait—"

"Love you and Dad…" And Felicity, too. That was why she needed to find the little girl's father. She clicked off Nikki's phone and handed it back to the female bodyguard. "Call Parker," she said. "Please."

Nikki's brown eyes narrowed as she studied Wendy's face. "I thought talking to your mom would make you feel better. It always does me."

Wendy shook her head. The talk with her mother had only made her feel worse. "It made me even more certain that my fears are right."

"That you're in love with Hart?" Nikki asked.

She was, but Wendy shook her head again. "That he's still in danger."

That damn feeling was back and so intense that it was tearing up Parker's insides. He reached for the already half-empty bottle of antacids on his desk. But just as he closed his hand around it, his cell began to ring.

Nikki…

That feeling intensified.

She was protecting the evidence tech—against his wishes. But Nikki's boss, who was also their brother Cooper, and the chief, had overruled him. Sure, Parker knew she was good. But he and Logan had spent too many years protecting their younger sister to entirely trust her protecting someone else.

His hand shook a little when he pressed the accept button on his cell. "What's wrong?"

He hoped nothing, but his gut was telling him differently. He knew he was right when the female voice on the phone wasn't his sister's but Wendy Thompson's.

"Parker?"

"Yes," he replied. "Is Nikki all right?"

"Yes," his sister answered. They must have had him on speaker.

"What's up?" he asked, curious about the conference call. One of them probably wanted to leave the hotel where he'd insisted they hole up.

After what had happened the last time she'd gone to a hotel to hide out, Wendy had been understandably nervous about going to another one. She'd worried that she might put other people in danger. She was incredibly selfless.

Like when she'd given up Hart as her bodyguard so that his daughter wouldn't lose him.

But now she asked, "Where's Hart?"

"Why?" He smiled. Maybe she wasn't as selfless as he'd thought. "Did you change your mind about having him as your bodyguard?"

Parker suspected Wendy's crush on the former RCPD detective was why she hadn't wanted Hart to protect her any longer—she'd been more concerned with protecting him.

"No, not at all," she said.

"See," Nikki chimed in. "She's happy with me as a bodyguard."

"She's one of the only ones," Parker teased his sister.

She cursed him just as teasingly.

Wendy Thompson lost her patience with them both. "I'm worried about Hart," she said. "He was supposed to be at the safe house with my parents this morning, but he hasn't shown up yet."

"That's my fault," Parker admitted.

He'd had to get permission from the chief to share the location of the safe house with Hart. At least Parker knew where this one was, though. Only the chief knew where he'd hidden Rosie Mendez and Clint Quarters. Of course, Parker's mother probably knew, too. He doubted Woodrow could keep anything from her—whether he wanted to or not.

"I couldn't tell him right away."

"You were keeping his daughter from him?" Wendy asked.

He could hear the recrimination in her voice. "I was keeping her, and your parents, safe," he reminded her. That was the priority over everything else. That nothing happened to the little girl and Wendy's parents.

"You have to make sure Hart's safe," she implored him. There was a strange urgency in her voice, as if she was having the same feeling that Parker was.

"And he should be," he said, trying to convince himself and his gut as much as he was her. "He's no longer protecting you."

He heard a gasp. He didn't know if it was Wendy's or Nikki's.

"Sorry," he said. "I hadn't meant that to sound harsh."

"It's true," Wendy said. "Or at least I thought it was…"

She definitely sounded as if she was feeling the same way he was. That Hart was not out of danger at all.

"What's going on?" he asked. "Why are you worried?"

"I keep thinking about the shooting at the hotel," she said. "When Hart got shot, I was right there. He fell and I was standing, giving the shooter a clear shot at me. He had the perfect opportunity to kill me, but he didn't."

"He was hurt," Nikki reminded her. "We saw blood at the scene."

"It'll take a while for the short-staffed lab to get back the DNA results," she said. "And for them to process the evidence from the explosion. That's the other thing bothering me. It's not like Luther Mills to use explosives."

"We figured this was a hired hit," Parker said, knowing Luther had the money to hire the best, like his sleazeball criminal lawyer.

"Yes," Wendy agreed. "But is that hired hit man after me or Hart?"

Parker reached for the bottle of antacids. His gut was nearly screaming at him again that something bad was going to happen. He'd been worried about Wendy and Nikki. Now he wondered, was it Hart who was in danger?

Hart had had a late start, but that wasn't what was keeping him from driving straight to that safe house and his daughter. He wasn't even reluctant because he was worried that Ben Thompson would be disappointed he'd broken his promise.

That bothered him, though.

He'd made a promise to a man he respected. But then he'd bailed because he'd got scared. Not of getting hurt physically.

But of getting hurt emotionally again.

He'd never felt about Monica the way he felt about Wendy. And his divorce had nearly destroyed him. What would happen if Wendy turned out to have the same attention span that Monica had had?

After all, she'd said that what they'd done was just sex to her, nothing more.

Just as it had been for Monica. Sex and nothing more because she hadn't known how to love. Just like his dad, who'd left him and his mom when he was young…just like Monica had left Felicity, for a lover.

If he fell for another woman…

Hell, he'd never really fallen for Monica, though. Not like he'd fallen for Wendy. So if Wendy lost interest in him the way Monica had, and turned to someone else, he wasn't sure he would survive that pain—that loss.

But he wasn't certain he was going to survive now.

No. Breaking his promise to Ben Thompson wasn't keeping him from the safe house. Hart was stalling because he'd noticed the tail shortly after he'd left the Payne Protection Agency. It wasn't a white van, but then, that had been abandoned in a parking lot. Hell, he wasn't even sure it was the same driver. That driver had been so good, he'd avoided detection several times.

This driver was a little too obvious, a little too desperate, to allow much more than a car or two between them.

When Hart pulled off onto a more remote road, the black sedan was the only one behind him.

Was this person like Terrance Gibbs, so frightened to disappoint Luther Mills that he would risk getting caught to do his bidding?

Hart had caught him following him. And because of that, he'd made certain he'd taken roads leading away from the safe house. There was no way he would let anyone follow him to his daughter and Wendy's parents. He wasn't able to protect her anymore, but at least he could protect them.

He also wanted to protect innocent bystanders, so he turned onto another street, one so untraveled that it wasn't paved. Hell, it was more dirt than gravel even. He didn't know where it was headed, but he didn't care.

Of course, if he was more familiar with the area, he might have been able to lead the sedan into a trap. He still might be able to even though this SUV, his personal one, wasn't souped up like the Payne Protection vehicles. His was all-wheel drive, though; the sedan was probably only front-wheel.

He sped up and the car sped up, as well. The driver didn't seem to care that he'd been made. He had to know that Hart wasn't going to lead him to the safe house now. But maybe he was so angry and so desperate that he had nothing to lose anymore. He made that clear when he accelerated so hard he rammed into the back bumper of the SUV.

Hart cursed. His vehicle definitely wasn't as good as the Payne Protection ones. It was lighter, the metal not reinforced. He had to grip the steering wheel tightly as he fought to keep the vehicle on the road. What gravel there was sprayed out behind his tires, striking the hood of the sedan and kicking up against the windshield. The glass cracked, obscuring Hart's view of the driver.

Who the hell was after him?

It felt personal now.

There was no one else in his vehicle, so it wasn't as if someone was only trying to get him out of the way to get to Wendy. If that were the case, she would have been shot at the hotel once he'd been hit and had fallen.

But the shooter had stopped shooting then. Had never even fired a shot at her.

No. Hart was the target.

The thought stunned him for a moment and he didn't see the curve until it was too late. He hit his brakes to slow down, but the tires hit a patch of slick mud. His SUV spun like he'd hit ice. Even though the vehicle was all-wheel drive, the tires couldn't grip the road.

The SUV slid off the road, tumbling as it struck the steep ditch. It rolled again, out of the ditch and into a stand of trees. Curses slipped through his lips as the impact jarred his wounded leg. But his leg was the least of his concerns right now. A branch had broken through the windshield, pushing the rearview mirror toward Hart until it struck his temple.

He blinked and tried to clear his vision, but everything had gone black.

Chapter 21

Luther stared through the shatterproof glass. Some years had passed since Parker Payne had been a vice cop, but the man didn't look any older than he had back then. Son of a bitch was too damn good-looking to age badly. But then, hopefully, he wouldn't age much more than he already was.

Luther picked up the handset, the twin to which Parker already clutched on the other side of the glass. "To what do I owe this pleasure?" he asked, his voice thick with sarcasm.

He'd been getting bored. While he pretty much had free rein of the jail, it was still jail. He couldn't come and go as he pleased, especially since Jocelyn Gerber had started checking out the guards at the jail. Everyone was so damn worried about being caught associating with him.

He'd started feeling a little lonely. Lonely enough that he welcomed a visit from anyone—even a damn Payne.

A grimace of disgust crossed Parker's stupidly handsome face. He wasn't as pleased with this visit as Luther was. "It's probably a waste of my time coming here…"

Luther would have a hell of a lot of time wasting away if he couldn't get the charges against him tossed out, preferably before the trial even started. That was coming up quick, so he had to make that happen. Soon. Of course, he already had a plan in motion.

Had old Parker got wind of that plan?

He studied the other man through the glass. "What do you want, Payne?"

And what was he willing to give up for it?

The eyewitness?

The evidence tech?

Luther might not need his help with that last one, though. He had a promising lead.

"I want the truth," Payne replied.

Luther snorted. "What? You think I don't know these visits are recorded? You think I'm going to give you some emotional confession you can use against me?"

Especially not when he was so close to eliminating at least one of his problems.

"I don't expect you to confess all your sins," Parker said, glancing at his watch. "I don't have that kind of time anyway."

"Smart-ass." That was the problem with the Paynes. They were too damn smart—for his good.

"I just want you to admit to one."

Luther snorted again. "Then you are wasting your time…" He started to pull the phone away from his ear.

"Wait!" Parker said, his deep voice vibrating with frustration.

He did seem to want this particular information. Badly.

Maybe he would be willing to pay for it.

"Whatever you want, you're going to have to pay for it," Luther said. "You know I've never given freebies."

That wasn't entirely true. When he wanted to hook someone, he gave freebies. Then once they were hooked, he owned them. Hell, he pretty much owned everyone in River City. Or he used to…

Luther could feel that control slipping away from him now. And he hated it. Most especially, he hated the people who were trying to take that control away from him. That was pretty much every damn person associated with his trial, including the Payne Protection Agency.

They better not stop him from getting rid of that damn evidence tech. But then, there weren't enough of them to stop him this time. That was what he'd learned from his previous failed attempts.

It wasn't the big, bold attacks that hadn't worked. It had been the crew he'd sent. He'd needed more experienced gun power.

"Luther," Parker said then shook his head. "I just need to know about the bomb and the hotel."

"What? Someone blew up a hotel?" He wanted no

part of that; shit like that got Homeland Security involved, got people talking terrorists and stuff. And then evidence wasn't all that important anymore. He would get shipped off somewhere that he couldn't get messages to the outside anymore. Or he'd get killed. He shook his head. "That ain't me. I don't mess with that shit."

"No bomb? Anywhere?" Parker asked.

"I told you. I don't mess with that shit."

"What about shooting up a hotel?" Parker asked.

"Hotel? What the hell are you trying to pin on me?" he asked angrily. He got mad enough when he was accused of the things he'd actually done. So maybe Parker needed to come back in a few hours after the evidence tech was eliminated...

Luther still wasn't going to blow up anything. But he had that other plan in motion. And if she was holed up where he'd heard...

A smirk tugged up the corners of his mouth. "Only thing I've heard about since I've been in here are some houses or apartments getting shot up," he replied. "And, of course, I had nothing to do with any of that."

Parker snorted but nodded. He didn't look any more pleased than he had when Luther had first walked into the visiting area. Obviously he hadn't told him what he'd wanted to hear.

"I ain't taking blame for something I haven't done."

Yet.

"You don't take blame for what you have done," Parker said with a heavy sigh. He started pulling the phone away from his ear.

"Wait!" Luther commanded. "Who got blown up? Who was at the hotel?"

Parker shook his head.

"Hey, I was honest with you," Luther said. And that was something he very rarely was. "Tell me."

"Hart Fisher."

Luther chuckled. "Someone blew up Hart Fisher."

Parker glared at him through the glass. "No. But someone tried."

Luther's chuckle turned to raucous laughter. Someone was helping him. Someone he didn't even know and, fortunately, didn't have to pay. When he finally stopped laughing, he noticed that Parker Payne was gone.

Now, if only the someone who tried blowing up Hart Fisher would take out the whole damn Payne Protection Agency...

Wendy hadn't wanted to call him; she hadn't wanted to seem desperate or like a stalker. But she hadn't been able to help herself, not as her niggling doubts had turned into full-fledged fears.

As it had before, after a few rings, the call went to his voice mail. She disconnected at the first sound of his deep voice as it sent a shiver rushing through her every time. Maybe he just didn't want to talk to her. But since she was using Nikki's phone, he wouldn't have even known she was the one calling him.

Wendy suspected there was another reason he wasn't picking up: he couldn't.

Hart was in danger; she just knew it somehow. They

had connected while he was protecting her, in more than a sexual way. In a deeper way…

Or so she'd thought until he'd walked away from her at the lab. Of course, he'd been angry with her for having him reassigned. She must have hurt his pride. But she'd done it for him and for Felicity. His daughter could not lose her father.

"No answer?" Nikki asked. Her beautiful face was tense with concern.

Wendy shook her head. "Can you call my mom back?"

Nikki nodded and pulled out her cell. After punching in a number, she handed it to Wendy.

"Is he there yet?" she anxiously asked the moment her father picked up the phone.

"Hart?" Ben asked. "Why the hell is he coming without you anyway? He promised he'd take care of you."

Since her father was swearing, he was obviously alone. "Dad, he's a single father. His daughter needs him more than I do."

She wasn't so certain about that. She needed him, too, even more than she'd realized.

"Well, he's not here," her father said, disapproval in his voice. "She's getting anxious waiting for him. She's missed him and you. That little girl has already got attached."

The fierce emotion in his voice made it clear that Felicity wasn't the only one who'd got attached. He'd fallen for the little girl, as well.

He admitted it when he asked, "Do you think Hart

will let us keep seeing her? Your mother will be devastated if she can't."

Wendy smiled. "Sure, Mom's the only one..."

"You would, too," her father said.

He was right.

But she wasn't worried now about what Hart would or would not allow. She didn't want her father to know what she was worried about, though, so she told him, "Hart's boss, Parker, said that he got a late start today. So it's not surprising he's not there yet."

"Then why did you call to see if he was?" her father asked. He was once again the football coach interrogating the team about their grades and their partying... and ferreting out the truth.

Nikki's cell beeped with an incoming call, saving Wendy from that interrogation. "I have to go, Dad," she said, grateful she'd had the chance to hear his voice. Her father's strong voice had made her feel a little stronger. "Love you."

He was saying he loved her, too, as she clicked Nikki's cell to take the other call. Since it was Nikki's brother and her cell, Wendy put it on speaker. "Yes?" she said. "Did you find him?"

"Um... Wendy?" Parker hedged.

She almost suspected he was stalling for time or determining how much to tell her. "I keep calling him," she said, "and he's not picking up. Have you tried?"

There was a long hesitation, a deep sigh and then, finally, an admission. "Yes...and no, he's not picking up..."

"You need to find him," she said.

"I know. That's why I called Nikki. I need her to tap into the GPS on Hart's vehicle or on his cell to see if she can pinpoint his location."

Nikki grabbed her laptop, opened it and called out, "I'm on it."

"You're worried, too," Wendy said. "Why? Did you figure out I was right about the bomb and the hotel shooting?"

"I don't have proof," Parker said. "But…"

"What?" Wendy prodded.

Nikki answered for her brother. "He has our mother's sixth sense all of a sudden." She sighed almost enviously. "Cooper got it, too, once he started his own franchise of Payne Protection."

"Sixth sense?" Wendy asked.

"They just know when something bad is going to happen," Nikki explained. Then her face flushed and she apologized. "I'm sorry. We don't know that anything at all has happened to Hart."

But Wendy knew—just like Parker did. Hart wasn't picking up her call, not because he didn't want to talk to her. But because he couldn't…

The buzzing was so loud Hart felt it as well as heard it. It reverberated throughout his aching head and forced him to pry open his eyes and peer around. As he did, his head swam with disorientation and dizziness. He blinked again and focused on his surroundings.

He was upside down, pinned between his seat and the airbag that had inflated over his steering wheel.

That airbag had probably saved his life. But he wasn't safe yet.

Where had the driver of the other vehicle gone? He couldn't see anything through the branches of the tree that had broken through his windshield. And he could hear only that intermittent buzzing.

It must have been his cell phone—wherever the hell it was. Then he noticed the flash of the screen. The cell was caught between the console and the passenger's seat, which had been squeezed tightly together in the crash. The phone wasn't broken, though, since it kept buzzing. Someone was calling him. Whoever it was couldn't help him now. He had to get the hell out of the wreckage and help himself.

He had just managed to free his seat belt when the first gun blast echoed and a bullet pinged off the under-carriage of the SUV. He pushed aside the broken glass and the branches and shoved his way through the wind-shield. Jagged glass and metal caught at his clothes, tearing them and scratching his skin. He didn't give a damn about scratches, though. He didn't want to get shot again.

His thigh was still throbbing and aching from his earlier gunshot wound. He certainly didn't want to get killed and leave Felicity alone. He had to escape—for his daughter.

And for Wendy...

He shouldn't have walked away from her. He should have stayed and kept his promise to her father—kept her safe. Hell, he should have just kept her.

He shouldn't have been such a damn coward when

he'd realized how he'd felt about her. He shouldn't have been so worried about getting hurt himself. He should have worried only about her getting hurt.

But maybe she was safer without him. Whoever was after him had to know he was alone in the SUV. Why were they still trying to kill him?

Once he scrambled through the branches and the glass, he was still beneath the wreckage—beneath the hood as the vehicle rested on the roof. Before edging out from under it, he reached for his holster. The snap had opened but, fortunately, his weapon hadn't fallen out this time like it had during the explosion.

He pulled out his gun and slipped off the safety. As he edged out from the wreckage on his back, he fired at whoever was firing at the undercarriage. He couldn't see anything, but he hoped the barrage of bullets would keep the guy from firing back.

Once he was clear of the wreck, he scrambled to his feet and headed into the woods as fast as he could move with his leg throbbing and aching. After a few minutes, he heard brush rustling as the shooter scrambled down the steep ditch in pursuit.

He smiled.

Hart had no idea where the hell he was, but he knew that at least he wasn't outnumbered as he had been at the Thompsons'.

This was a fair fight. Not that Hart intended to fight fair.

Chapter 22

Parker hurled the empty bottle of antacids in the trash can. No matter how many he took, he hadn't eased that sick feeling in his gut. But he didn't think it was just Hart who was in danger anymore.

He kept replaying that jailhouse meeting in his mind. Until Parker had brought up the bomb and the hotel, Luther had been relaxed. Like he hadn't had a care in the world even though he was about to go on trial for murder.

He'd been more concerned about getting blamed for something he hadn't done than going down for something he had done. Like he was pretty damn confident that trial would never happen...

Wendy had assured the chief that the evidence was safe. That Luther couldn't get to it.

But what about her? Or the eyewitness?

Hell, even Parker didn't know where Rosie Mendez was. So it had to be Wendy that Luther thought he could get to. She had refused to leave River City like Rosie had. So he'd found her a hotel with higher security than the one she'd stayed in with Hart, and he'd implemented their own security system with Nikki being in the room with her and a few other guards in the parking lot.

Was that enough if Luther sent the kind of firepower after her like he had at her parents' house? Of course, the Thompson house had been easy to find. They were in the damn phone book.

How would Luther know which hotel Parker had booked for Wendy? How would he even know she was at a hotel? But then, Luther had people everywhere. That was the problem.

Parker picked up his cell but hesitated over punching in Nikki's contact. She'd promised to call him once she'd tracked down Hart. And he didn't want to disrupt her.

But he felt compelled to send out a text to all the guards protecting Wendy. He included Hart, as well. Maybe his gut had misled him about Hart. Maybe he was fine and just out of cell phone coverage.

When he got within range again, he would receive the text Parker sent out to the others.

Be on full alert. Met with Mills. Certain he has an attack planned...

Would full alert be enough? Would Payne Protection be able to save Wendy?

* * *

Wendy glanced down at Nikki's cell as the text flashed on the screen. What did it mean?

Who did he think Luther was going to attack? Her or one of the others? Everyone involved with the trial had been threatened, not just her.

Hell, even someone not involved had been threatened. The judge's daughter. Maybe Luther thought he could use Bella Holmes against the judge to get the evidence thrown out. If that was going to happen, then he didn't need to take Wendy out.

Because she didn't know for certain that warning was about her, she didn't draw Nikki's attention to it. She didn't want to call Nikki's attention from her laptop, where she worked feverishly to find Hart's whereabouts.

That was more important—making sure that Hart was okay. She'd thought she was doing the right thing, for him and his daughter, when she'd asked for Parker to reassign him.

But at least when he'd been protecting her, he'd had backup. There were always other bodyguards around. Now he was off somewhere on his own, alone and vulnerable.

And even if he didn't get hurt protecting her, Wendy would still hold herself responsible. She should have figured out sooner that the shooter at the hotel hadn't been firing at her.

He'd been aiming at Hart. If he'd been working for Luther, he would have taken a shot at her—no matter how badly he might have been hurt from Hart shooting him. Because nobody dared to cross or disappoint Luther Mills.

So if he wasn't working for Luther, who the hell was he working for? Hart had made a lot of arrests before he'd left River City PD. He'd probably made more than his share of enemies, more than just Luther Mills.

So who was after him? Had they got him?

Wendy's heart and head pounded with fear. Despite Parker's warning text, that fear wasn't for her own safety. She was worried only about Hart and about what losing him would do to his young daughter.

And to her...

She loved him. So much...

Even though he didn't return her feelings, she should have told him, so that he would have known why she'd no longer wanted him protecting her. Because now she might never get the chance to tell him how she felt...

Wendy didn't have that sixth sense the Payne family seemed to possess, but she just *knew* that Hart was not okay.

Hart was not okay. He was furious. And disgusted. Whoever the hell was shooting at him was not the person who'd fired at him outside the hotel. Of course, he'd already figured it out—from the poor job the guy had done tailing him—that this was not the same person who'd driven the white van.

That man had obviously been a professional.

So what had happened to him?

If someone wanted Hart dead, that was the person who could have done the job. Not this one...

Hart waited until the dull click of the empty chamber before he stepped out of the trees that had absorbed all the bullets fired at him. With a weary sigh, he pointed his gun at the shooter. He didn't have time for this—whatever the hell this was...

"Put it down," he ordered the man. "On the ground."

The guy jumped at Hart's sudden appearance and the weapon slipped through his grasp. He glanced up at Hart and the hood of his sweatshirt fell back.

Hart gasped in surprised recognition.

"Bruno?" He'd only met the Frenchman once when Monica had brought her fiancé with her when she'd said goodbye to Felicity. His ex had chosen Bruno over her daughter. But then, she'd never paid Felicity much attention anyway. "What the hell are you trying to do?"

The man's face flushed with anger, his small dark eyes wild with desperation.

Hart reached out, grasped one of the man's thin shoulders and shook him. He asked again. "What the hell are you doing?"

Bruno Lemieux was no killer.

"I want you gone!" Bruno exclaimed.

"Gone?" Hart repeated. None of this made any sense.

It definitely hadn't been Bruno who'd planted the bomb or tried to drive him off the road with the white van.

"You're supposed to be dead," Bruno said. All the anger and frustration was his now. "I hired someone. He was supposed to take care of you. But after you shot him, he quit."

Wendy had seen the blood and directed a tech to

collect it even though she'd wanted to test it herself. Hart probably should have let her process that scene. Maybe she could have figured all this out, because Bruno wasn't doing a very damn good job of explaining anything to Hart.

"Or he tried to quit..." the Frenchman murmured, as if he didn't know what he was saying anymore.

Hart had a sick feeling that he was wrong. Maybe Bruno Lemieux was a killer now. He must have killed the man he'd hired to kill Hart. But why the hell did he want Hart *gone*?

"So I have to get rid of you," Bruno continued. He moved as if to reach for the gun he'd dropped. Even though it was empty, Hart kicked it away into the brush.

"Why do you want to get rid of me?" Hart asked him. "I have nothing to do with you and your wife."

"You have everything," Bruno said, and his voice shook with frustration. "You have her daughter."

Felicity was everything. Or she had been until Wendy had entered Hart's life—and his heart. How the hell had he thought he wouldn't be able to fall for her? She was so amazing and not just at her job and with her family but with Felicity, too. She already had a better connection with the child than her own mother had.

So what the hell was Bruno babbling about?

"Monica is miserable without her," the guy declared.

Hart snorted. "Yeah, right..."

"She misses her and wants her back," Bruno insisted. "But she said there is no way you would ever let her even have visitation with her daughter. So that is why you have to die. So she gets full custody."

Hart shook his head. "There is no way in hell that Monica wants full custody. She never wanted to be a mother. She never spent any time with her. Why would she want her?"

Bruno's eyes blurred with confusion. "But that is what she said…"

"To kill me?"

Monica hadn't been angry with him. In fact, she'd acted like she pitied him for having to be a full-time father. She wouldn't have wanted him dead because then she would have to actually take responsibility for her child.

Bruno shook his head. "She said that is why she keeps going off by herself. She needs to be alone to nurse her lonely heart."

Realization dawned and Hart began to laugh.

The smaller man bristled. "You think it's funny that she hurts? No wonder she left you."

"I divorced her," Hart corrected him. "Because she was constantly having affairs. Monica does not go off alone to nurse her lonely heart. She goes off with whatever willing male she finds."

Bruno shook his head, his small eyes looking even more desperate. Probably because he knew Hart spoke the truth.

"I hate to break it to you, buddy, but she's cheating on you."

Bruno shook his head again. It was clear that he knew; his face flushed and tears began to pool in those beady eyes.

Hart almost felt sorry for him. But not sorry enough

that he didn't slug him. When Bruno dropped unconscious to the ground, Hart shook his hand. His knuckles were probably going to swell. It had been worth it for the guy wasting his damn time—and for putting Wendy in danger.

While the hired hit man hadn't taken that shot at her, he could have hurt her in the explosion. Or with the white van. And Luther Mills wanting her dead had already put her in enough damn danger.

Hart backtracked to his SUV. Seeing the damage to his personal vehicle made him wish he'd hit Bruno even harder. Damn idiot.

He kicked in the passenger's window and reached inside, trying to fish out his cell phone. He needed to call someone to cart the idiot off to jail. He could have fished out Bruno's phone and used it, but he also wanted to see who had been calling him.

When he finally snaked his cell out of the wreckage, the first thing he saw on the screen was a text.

Be on full alert. Met with Mills. Certain he has an attack planned...

Parker's warning chilled Hart. While Bruno had sent the gunman to the hotel and had probably had him plant the bomb, too, Luther had been responsible for the attack at the Thompsons' home.

Had he planned something like that again?

Hart shivered as he remembered how close he had come to losing everything he cared about: his daughter.

And Wendy.

Those two gunmen had made it into the house, had nearly killed her. Would she escape unscathed this time, too?

Hart had no doubt that this attack was meant to take out Wendy. After the retired lab tech had failed to find the evidence, Luther must have learned that Wendy was the only link to it. And maybe he thought killing her would eliminate the evidence, as well.

She'd assured the chief, and the assistant district attorney, that it would get to them if something happened to her.

Luther might have been willing to take the chance that wouldn't happen, though. Or he was confident that his informants in the River City PD and in the district attorney's office would take out the evidence once it was received.

Either way, Wendy was in danger. It didn't matter how many bodyguards she had—Hart wanted to be there for her. To protect her...and to love her.

He'd taken off because he was afraid of getting hurt. But now he realized that nothing would cause him more pain than Wendy being hurt—or worse.

He could not lose her. Not now, when he'd finally realized how damn much he loved and needed her.

He scrambled up the bank to where Bruno had left his vehicle, engine running, on the road. He must have figured he'd be able to shoot Hart and make a fast getaway.

Hart pulled open the driver's door to find bullets spilled across the passenger's seat and console. No wonder it had taken the man so long to start shooting. He'd struggled to even load the gun.

If Hart left him before making sure the police arrived, Bruno might get away. But his getaway wouldn't be fast. The guy would have to walk for miles to find any civilization. Hart would call the police once he was on his way back to River City.

And Wendy.

He only hoped that he made it in time to help, to save her if necessary, like she had just saved him. Again.

As he spun the car into a turn and headed away from the wreckage of the SUV, he looked at his call log. While some of the missed calls had been from Parker, most of them had been from Nikki, who was supposed to be protecting Wendy.

It had been that buzzing that had woken him up. If he hadn't regained consciousness before Bruno had finished loading his gun, the guy might have actually got rid of him like he'd wanted.

Hart pressed his foot hard on the accelerator of the sedan. He could have called Nikki to check on Wendy. He could have had the female bodyguard tell Wendy that he was coming. But she'd claimed she didn't want him to protect her anymore. So she probably wouldn't let Nikki tell him where she was.

He needed to talk to someone who would tell him. But even once he learned her location, he knew he might not make it in time.

Only Luther knew when he'd planned his attack.

It could already be happening. And, in that case, Hart didn't want to call and distract anyone.

Everyone needed to be focused on keeping Wendy safe.

Chapter 23

Luther glanced up at the clock on the TV room wall. It should be happening *now*.

It would all be over soon.

Once Wendy Thompson was dead, that evidence would show up. She was too smart to not have a plan in place in case something happened to her. She'd seen that crime scene; she knew what he did to people like Javi—people who tried to take him down. When the evidence showed up wherever she'd sent it, probably at the district attorney's office, he would have it destroyed just like he was having her destroyed.

He started laughing, even though the show on the TV screen wasn't the least bit funny. The show playing in Luther's mind was, though.

It was the one in which Wendy Thompson died, along

with as many of the Payne Protection Agency body-guards as they could take out. With most of his crew either in jail or dead, he'd had to reach out to another gang—in another city. They'd needed some serious incentive to help him, though, so he'd offered one reward for taking out the evidence tech and another for every damn bodyguard who was killed.

It might wind up costing him. Big. But it would cost the Paynes a hell of a lot more.

And it would cost Wendy Thompson everything—just like he'd warned her. The self-righteous bitch should have heeded his warning.

Wendy probably should have heeded that warning from Parker. She felt a twinge of guilt for not interrupting Nikki when the text had come in from her brother. But Parker had sent it over an hour ago and nothing had happened yet.

Surely he'd just been overreacting to his meeting with Luther Mills. Maybe that Payne sixth sense wasn't as reliable as they all believed it was. Or maybe Luther had gone after the judge's daughter instead. Or maybe Hart was the only one in danger right now.

There could only be one reason he hadn't made it to the safe house. Something had happened to him.

Something *bad*.

Her heart ached with her loss and with Felicity's. If the little girl lost her father, she would be inconsolable.

As would Wendy...

Nikki glanced up from her computer.

Wendy's pulse quickened and she anxiously asked, "Did you find him?"

"He's using his personal vehicle," Nikki reminded her. "So I had to do some motor vehicle record searches to find it and his vehicle identification number before I could hack into his GPS."

"But you did?" Wendy asked hopefully.

Nikki nodded, but her brow was furrowed. Her teeth sank into her bottom lip as if she didn't want to share everything she'd learned.

"What is it?" Wendy asked, her hope beginning to fade at the look on her bodyguard's beautiful face. "Tell me..."

"It recorded that it had been in an accident earlier today."

Wendy suspected that whatever had happened had been no accident. "The guy in the white van—he must have come after Hart again."

"It was a single-vehicle crash," Nikki said.

So Hart had wrecked on his own? She didn't believe it. She'd ridden with him; he was too good a driver, even when someone was trying to force him off the road.

"You know where it is, right?"

Nikki nodded.

Wendy jumped up and grabbed her jacket from where she'd draped it across the bed. "We need to go there."

Nikki wasn't moving.

"What?" Wendy asked because she knew there was more.

"I tapped into the GPS on his phone, too," Nikki said. "It's not with his vehicle."

Wendy's head began to pound like her heart had already been pounding. "So maybe he got a ride with someone after his vehicle crashed—" Her heart stopped beating for a moment altogether before resuming at a frantic pace. "Or in an ambulance."

Nikki reached for the cell phone she'd left on the table where Wendy had been sitting. She glanced at the screen. "Parker sent a warning text…"

As soon as she said it, gunfire rang out.

Outside the window, there were flashes of light. Then the window shattered, spraying glass into the room and over Nikki.

Wendy's pang of guilt became an overwhelming stabbing sensation. "Are you okay?" she anxiously asked her.

"Get down!" Nikki shouted. If she was hurt, she didn't betray any pain or fear as she pulled her weapon and turned toward the window, returning fire.

Wendy drew her weapon, too.

Nikki pulled back just as more gunfire exploded. Bullets came through the broken window and embedded in the wall behind Wendy.

"How the hell do they know which room we're in?" Nikki murmured.

Wendy thought it was a rhetorical question until she saw the cell pressed to Nikki's ear.

"Is anyone hurt in the parking lot?" the female bodyguard said into the phone. Her face was tight and pale. She was finally afraid but it wasn't for herself.

Wendy remembered that Nikki's husband was out there. The blond giant of a man—Lars Ecklund.

"Is he hurt?" she asked.

Nikki shook her head as she pulled the cell away from her ear. She hadn't put it on speaker. Maybe she didn't want Wendy to know how bad their situation was. But she knew it was bad when the auburn-haired beauty said, "We have to get the hell out of here."

Still crouched below the window, Nikki headed toward the door. As she pulled it open, they heard the ding of the elevator and a curse slipped through the bodyguard's lips. "Hurry!"

Wendy, crouching low, rushed into the hall with Nikki. She pulled the door shut behind her and they ran down the corridor, away from the sound of the elevator doors whooshing open. There was a stairwell at their end. Nikki pushed open those doors. But they could hear the heavy fall of footsteps on the stairs, of people coming up from below.

Nikki pressed a finger to her lips for Wendy to be quiet. Then she pointed up. They couldn't go down. So they had to go up.

Wendy's legs shook, and not just from exertion, as she ran up those stairs. Fear gripped her. Fear for herself and for Nikki. It was a bad idea going up. It left them nowhere to go but down, from the roof of a twelve-story building.

She was also afraid for Felicity and Hart. If something happened to her and Nikki, maybe nobody would find Hart. And he needed to be with his daughter.

She needed them both. So she had to fight to survive, for them as much as for herself. She pushed open the door at the top of the stairwell and stepped onto the roof. Nikki came out behind her and shoved the door shut. Then she looked around, trying to find something to prop against it.

Wendy saw a pipe sticking out of the roof and worked quickly, her hands shaking, to spin it loose from the threads holding it in place. When it was free, Nikki pulled it from her hands and shoved it through the door handle. Just as she did, the door shuddered as a body struck it.

The pipe held but it wasn't that thick. It might give out eventually. Then what would they do?

They had no place to go. They were trapped. And from the way the door was shaking, there was more than one body slamming into it. Probably more than two.

So they were outnumbered, which meant they were also outgunned.

Hart ducked low as his windshield exploded. It wasn't branches coming through it this time but bullets. He pressed harder on the accelerator and kept going, ramming into the body of the shooter.

The guy flew over the hood and then the roof.

Apparently, Hart had found the right hotel. Parker had told him which one when he'd called to find out where the hell Wendy was. But Hart hadn't known for certain which street it was on—just that it was near the River City airport.

He drew his weapon, glad now that he hadn't wasted any more bullets on Bruno as gunfire exploded all around the lot. Like at the Thompsons', the perimeter guards had come under siege first. But he couldn't be certain that none of Luther's hired guns hadn't already made it inside the hotel.

He slammed Bruno's rented sedan into a van parked near one of the Payne Protection SUVs. More gunfire exploded as guys scrambled out of the van. They dropped to the pavement as the Payne bodyguards advanced on it.

He didn't know if they'd been shot or if they'd just had the sudden sense to surrender before they got shot.

A weapon pointed at him through the driver's window. "What the hell…?" Lars Ecklund murmured as he lowered the barrel of his gun. "I thought you'd gone missing."

"I had," Hart admitted. "Where is she?"

"With Nikki," Lars grimly replied, jerking his head at the hotel.

Hart didn't have to ask which room. He saw the broken glass on the sixth floor. "How the hell did they know?"

Lars cursed and shook his head. "How the hell does Luther Mills know anything…?" His voice trailed off as he bounded toward the building.

Hart shoved open the driver's door and hurried past the other bodyguards who were dealing with the shooters on the ground. Lars's legs were longer, but Hart caught up with him at the lobby entrance. He was about to ask if any gunmen had made it inside when he saw the fallen security guards.

He cursed.

Were they already too late?

If Wendy and Nikki were trapped in a hotel room, they had no place to go.

"I called her. I warned her," Lars said, his voice gruff with emotion. "She got out. Nikki's good. I'm sure they got out." He sounded like he was trying real hard to convince himself of that.

Hart wasn't so sure. "If they got out, where the hell would they go?" He stepped back out of the lobby and peered around the building. The only movement was in the parking lot, where the guards took down all the shooters.

Then there was a sudden whoosh of air and a dark shadow fell across Lars's face and then Hart's. Seconds later, something struck the sidewalk near them. A body.

They rushed over to it. The impact with the ground had done significant damage, but it was apparently a male.

"The roof," they said together.

The women had made it to the roof. That wasn't any safer than being locked in a hotel room, though. They had no place to go there, either, but down, like this body had come.

An image flashed through Hart's mind of Wendy landing on the sidewalk.

He flinched as pain gripped his heart. He could not let that happen. What the hell had he been thinking when he'd walked away from her lab?

Why had he trusted anyone else to keep her safe?

Because he hadn't trusted her not to break his heart?

He'd never been as angry or scared as he was now. But he was angry at himself. He'd been such an idiot. Such a coward...

He heard gunfire coming from a distance, coming

from up on the roof. How many of Luther's crew had made it up there to the women?

Lars and Hart rushed through the lobby. There were no elevators at the lobby level. It looked like they'd all stopped on the twelfth floor. And he knew...

There were a lot of hit men, enough that they'd needed all the elevators. Even if both women were armed, they were drastically outgunned.

He and Lars ran toward the stairwell and bounded up the steps as fast as they could. But they had so many floors to go and no way of knowing what they would find when they reached the roof.

Would they be able to save the women they loved? Or would they be too late?

Chapter 24

They had rushed out of the hotel room so quickly that they hadn't much ammunition with them. So Wendy and Nikki had had to make every bullet count.

But there were too many...

Too many men and not enough bullets.

Once she heard the click of the empty chamber, Wendy closed her eyes and braced herself for the worst. As she'd feared, the barrage of gunfire increased in intensity. She heard the blast of Nikki's gun; she must have had more magazines on her. But then she stopped.

All of it stopped.

Wendy sucked in a breath. Was she the only one who had survived? Or was she dead, too?

Before she could open her eyes, strong hands closed around her arms. Then she was lifted. Carried. She could have tried playing dead, but she knew she was alive from the wild pounding of her heart.

When she opened her eyes, she saw why her pulse had leaped and why her skin tingled. Hart was carrying her toward the open door to the stairwell.

"You're alive," she murmured.

Or had she joined him wherever he'd gone after he'd died? Were they both dead?

"You, too," he said as he glanced down at her.

"Where are you taking her?" Nikki called after them.

Wendy peered over his shoulder to see her bodyguard. Nikki moved away from her husband, who'd had his big arms wrapped tightly around her. Wendy's breath shuddered out with relief that the other woman had survived, too. If anything had happened to Nikki, Wendy never would have forgiven herself for not sharing Parker's warning.

Obviously that Payne sixth sense was not a myth. It really existed. It really worked.

"I'm her bodyguard now," Nikki called after Hart.

He kept walking. Hell, he was nearly running despite his wounded leg.

"Hart!" Wendy exclaimed. "You need to put me down. You're hurt."

"I'm fine now," he said. And he certainly seemed fine as he descended that first flight of stairs with no trouble despite carrying her. Then he pushed open a door with his shoulder and headed to the elevators.

Once the doors closed on them, she tried again to wriggle down, but he held her tightly and as effortlessly as if she was the rag doll his daughter loved so much. The one she thought Winnie looked like…

"You're putting too much extra weight on your leg," she protested.

"You're fine."

She wasn't as light as that rag doll or Felicity. He shouldn't have been carrying her.

"What are you doing?" she asked.

"Taking you someplace safe."

In the parking lot, he had to convince another body-guard to give up an SUV.

He drove off with her, passing police cars and ambulances heading for the hotel.

"Shouldn't we go back?" she asked. "Won't we have to give a report?"

"To who?" Hart asked, his voice gruff with frustration. "One of Luther's moles? He keeps finding out where you are."

"I don't think he was behind the shooting at the other hotel," she said. "And neither does Parker."

"I know he wasn't," Hart acknowledged. "That was my ex's new husband."

She gasped. "Shooting at us?"

"That was the assassin Bruno, Monica's husband, hired," Hart said.

Wendy realized now how his vehicle had crashed. "You had a run-in with him."

He nodded. "It's over now."

"Was she behind it?" she asked.

Hart grunted. "I'm a bad judge of character," he said.

"But no, I wouldn't have married someone capable of murder."

She flinched as she thought of all the people she might have just killed. Her head pounded so hard, she closed her eyes.

A hand gripped hers, squeezed reassuringly. "There's a big difference between self-defense and murder," he reminded her. "Whatever happened up there on that roof? That was self-defense."

She knew that, of course. But it didn't lessen her guilt that much.

"It was you or them," he said. His grip tightened slightly before he released her hand.

She opened her eyes but didn't recognize the scenery moving quickly past the windows of the SUV. "Where are you taking me?" she asked.

"Someplace safe…"

She tensed. "Don't take me where my parents and Felicity are," she protested. "I don't want to put them in danger." She didn't want to put him in danger, either. She should have fought harder to free herself when he'd carried her off the roof and out of the hotel.

But she hadn't wanted to get away from him. She'd wanted to cling to him just as she had, her arms linked tightly around his neck. That was selfish, though, and she felt another pang of guilt.

"Felicity is expecting you," she said. "You need to go to her."

"I will," he said. "I called her while I was on my way to the hotel. I told her that I was going to try to convince Winnie to come with me."

Tears rushed to her eyes. She closed them tightly, trying to hold them back. She was afraid that if she started, she might not stop.

Wendy cleared her throat and said, "You shouldn't have done that. I can't go…"

The vehicle stopped. Maybe he'd finally listened.

She opened her eyes, but he was stepping out of the SUV. Then he came around to her side of the vehicle to open her door. She peered around him at the small house behind him.

"Where are we?" she asked.

They couldn't have already arrived at the safe house. Parker had made it sound as if it was far from River City. And Hart had not been driving that long.

"My mother's house," he said.

"But she's dead…"

He nodded. "I've had it rented out since she passed away," he said. "The last tenants just moved out and the new ones aren't moving in until the first of next month." He pulled a ring of keys from his pocket as they walked up the sidewalk to the front door.

Why had he taken her to his condo earlier instead of here, then?

"I would have brought you here earlier," he said, answering her unspoken question. "But it was actually being fumigated and cleaned for the new tenants."

Unlike the lie she'd told her parents.

When the door opened, she could smell chemicals. Fortunately, it was the scent of carpet cleaners rather than pesticides. They could stay here.

But they shouldn't…

Hart needed to get to his daughter. Felicity needed him. But then he pulled her into his arms and lowered his head to hers and need overwhelmed her. Her desire for him—her love—was too intense for her to deny.

Just a short while ago she'd been worried that he was dead. That she would never be able to tell him how she felt. Now that she had the opportunity, the words, along with the emotion, stuck in her throat.

She was scared. She'd survived a rooftop shoot-out with desperate gunmen. But she was more scared now—with Hart—than she'd been then.

She was afraid that he did not return her feelings. At least, not her love…

He certainly shared her passion as he lifted her again. Even as he carried her, he kept his mouth on hers, kissing her deeply. His shoulder struck a doorjamb, jarring her. He nearly dropped her but then he tightened his arms around her again.

She giggled even as she clutched at his broad shoulders.

Then he was dropping her—onto a bed, though.

She settled against the soft mattress with a sigh. "It's a furnished house…"

"They're short-term tenants, just here on assignment," he said. "They need it furnished."

She didn't care why there was a bed. She was just grateful that there was one. She was even more grateful that he was there.

That he was alive.

And so was she…

Adrenaline rushed through her. She'd come so close

to death now—too many times—that she had to celebrate life. She had to celebrate love.

Even though she was too scared to tell him about her feelings, she showed him.

With her kiss…

With her touch…

She ran her fingers along the fly of his jeans, which strained from his erection. As she released the button and lowered the zipper, his breath hissed out like the rasp of the metal sliding down.

Then she freed him from his jeans and his boxers and wrapped her fingers around him.

He groaned. A low, intense groan, as if he was in pain. The tension must have been wound as tightly inside him as it was inside her. But, instead of seeking his release, he pulled her hand from him and focused on her.

He removed her clothes quickly, as quickly as he'd removed her from the crime scene at the hotel.

And, just like then, she got carried away.

But now it was on a tide of passion. It swept through her from her lips, as he kissed them, to the tips of her nipples, which he teased with his tongue as he moved down her body to her very core. His finger touched her there, teasing her to the brink of madness.

He moved his mouth even lower, his tongue flicking over the most sensitive part of her. She arched off the bed as an orgasm overcame her.

Then he was there, moving between her legs. While she'd panted for breath, he'd donned a condom. So he was sheathed when he eased inside her. And she was so ready for him.

Despite the release he'd just given her, the tension built again with each stroke. He lowered his head to hers and kissed her passionately as he moved deeply inside her.

The ache that had been in her heart from missing him was finally filled, like he filled her. She felt closer to him—connected—in a way that went beyond the physical. When she came again, he came with her, their bodies shuddering, their hearts beating frantically and their names on each other's lips.

When he slipped away to clean up, Wendy felt the ache begin again because she knew she had to let him go. He was already missing his daughter and Felicity was missing him. Wendy couldn't keep him from his child any longer, and if he tried to protect her until the trial, he risked dying—like so many had died at the hotel—and then he would be away from his daughter forever.

Wendy could not do that to the child or the man she loved.

Hart left the water running when he answered his cell. He didn't want to disturb Wendy with his conversation in case she'd fallen asleep again after they'd made love.

At least that was what it had been for him. Making love…

Had it only been sex for her, like she'd claimed?

Hart was beginning to have his suspicions about that, though.

The running water made it hard for him to hear his

caller, until Parker shouted his name. The cell fairly vibrated with the anger in his boss's voice.

"Yes," Hart replied.

"Where the hell are you?" Parker asked. "You can't just take back an assignment I took you off."

Hart's lips curved into a grin. He hadn't just taken the assignment back. He'd taken the woman. And he never intended to return her, if he could convince her to give him a chance.

Back at the hotel, he'd worried that he had missed that chance. He'd worried that he had let his fear cost him a future for her and a future for them.

Not just him and Wendy but for Felicity, too.

He'd been such a damn fool.

"Nobody will keep her safer than I will," Hart vowed. And not just until the trial was over, but for the rest of their lives.

"No!" a female voice chimed in.

It wasn't Nikki, defending her efforts to protect Wendy, who made the protest. It hadn't come through the cell phone. It had come from the woman standing in the open door to the bathroom.

She had got dressed already—while he stood naked before her, in more ways than one. He wanted to give her his heart. But she held his keys instead, gripped tightly in her hand.

Had she intended to sneak out on him?

Hart clicked off the cell phone even as Parker was sputtering, demanding to know what was going on. He wanted to find that out for himself first.

"What the hell are you doing?" he asked. "Were you leaving?"

She nodded.

"Why?"

Had he waited too long to tell her how he felt? Had he blown his chance?

Or maybe she really didn't care about him at all anymore. Maybe it had just been lust and sex between them as she'd claimed.

"You can't be my bodyguard," she told him.

"Why?"

She'd lowered her gaze as if she couldn't meet his eyes. And she seemed to be staring at the bandage wrapped around his thigh. Some blood had leaked through and stained the gauze a dark crimson. She murmured, "Because it's too dangerous."

He patted the bandage. "This wasn't because of you. Or even because of Luther Mills." Though he wouldn't have put it past that bastard. "What happened with the bomb and the shooting at the first hotel...that was Bruno."

She shook her head. "It's still too dangerous. Look at what nearly happened at my parents' house. You could have been killed then."

"I would have been," he agreed, "if you hadn't saved my life."

She met his gaze now and her eyes glistened with the tears she was furiously fighting back, her lashes fluttering as she blinked. "It's too risky," she said.

"That's what I thought, too," he admitted.

"The assignment?" she asked.

He shook his head. "You. I thought it was too risky falling for you."

She sucked in a breath and her green eyes widened with shock. "What?"

"I'm sorry," he said. "I was letting what happened with Monica affect me."

She flinched. "You must have loved her very much."

He shook his head again. "I didn't know her. Not the real her. And by the time I did, Felicity was already on the way. I couldn't abandon my child."

"That's why I don't want you as my bodyguard—"

He stepped closer and pressed his finger across her lips. "I know," he said. "And that's why I'm so damn sorry."

Her brow furrowed. "I don't understand…"

"You're nothing like Monica. You're as selfless as she is selfish," he said. "You gave up the best damn bodyguard with Payne Protection…" He cracked a grin, unable to keep a straight face at the outlandish claim. "Well, the best damn bodyguard for you," he amended. "Because you were worried that I would get hurt."

"You're all Felicity has," she reminded him, some of those tears brimming over and sliding down her beautiful face.

He cupped her jaw in one hand and wiped away the tears with the other. As he did, his fingers shook slightly. "No. I'm not all she has anymore. She has you. She has Winnie…"

"I don't want to put her in danger, either," Wendy said. "Especially not her…"

He smiled, knowing that at long last his daughter

would have the love of a mother. Wendy would love his child like she was hers, too.

And he hoped that soon she would be.

"Don't worry," he said. "I think I have a plan for how we can all be together and be safe. You just have to trust me."

"I've been told I'm too trusting," she said.

He smiled wider. "That's not true. Or you wouldn't have hidden that evidence."

She nodded.

"I need you to trust me," he said. "Like I trust you... with my heart."

"What are you saying?" she asked. She had gone very tense and still.

"I'm not doing a very damn good job, but I'm trying to express my feelings," he explained.

"By comparing me to your ex?" she asked.

He shook his head. "There is no comparison." But she'd freaked him out when she'd said that what they'd done was just sex. "And I should have realized that I could trust you with my heart. You won't betray me. Or abandon Felicity."

In fact, she had been willing to give him up for his daughter.

"You're the most amazing woman I've ever met," he said. "And I love you..."

Chapter 25

Wendy couldn't believe what Hart had said. He couldn't love her. But he seemed intent on proving that he did—when he made love to her all over again.

And it was definitely love. Not sex…

The way he kissed her…

The way he touched her…

And most especially the way he stared at her…

She had thought he would never look at her like that, with such a look of love. That look intensified as he moved inside her, joining their bodies. They moved as one, slowly driving each other out of their minds.

Then the pleasure crashed over Wendy, and she felt as if he'd driven her out of her body. It went limp and boneless, and she collapsed against his chest, which heaved as he panted for breath.

His finger stroked down her spine. "What about you?" he asked. "Was that just sex? Should I have no expectations?"

She smiled and he must have been able to feel it because he tickled her ribs. She squirmed against him and confessed, "It's love. I love you."

"It's not just lust?" he asked, his body tensing against her, not with passion now but with fear.

She remembered why he'd fought his feelings for her. He hadn't wanted her to hurt him.

She tipped her head up so her gaze met his. She wanted him to see the look in her eyes, the same that was in his. She loved him.

"It started out that way," she admitted. "I thought you were hot. And when your arrests piled up, I was impressed with your work ethic and your brain. And when I saw you with Felicity... I fell so hard for you."

His breath shuddered out in relief. "She's going to be so thrilled to see you. We should get dressed and get going. We could get there by morning."

"Are you sure she will be safe?" she asked.

He nodded. "Will you trust me like I asked?"

"I do trust you," she said. "With my life and with my heart." And she knew she could trust him with his daughter. He would keep all of them safe. "I love you, Hart Fisher."

He kissed her. "And I love you..."

Hart had thought his heart was too damaged to love anyone but his daughter. But he knew now that wasn't true. Monica had only hurt his pride and his ability to trust.

His heart was just fine and it continued to grow as he loved more. He loved Wendy so much, and he loved her parents, too.

Even though her father was once again pointing a gun at him...

He held up his hands. "No need for a shotgun wedding," he told Ben Thompson. "I freely want to marry your daughter."

"Maybe you should ask her first," Wendy remarked as she stepped around him and hugged her father.

Her dad clasped her closely, lifting her up and swinging her around like she was as little as Felicity. "There's my girl," he said. Over her red hair, he met Hart's gaze, and his eyes were filled with tears. "You kept your promise. You kept her safe."

"You kept yours, too," Hart said. He could see Felicity through the sliding doors that opened onto a fenced backyard. She was playing with Margaret, apparently making mud pies on a picnic table.

Wendy spotted her, too, and wriggled from her father's embrace. She pulled open the sliders and stepped into the backyard.

"Winnie!" Felicity yelled. She launched herself at Wendy, getting mud in her hair and on her face as she wrapped her arms around Wendy's neck.

Monica would have yelled at her for getting her dirty. Wendy laughed and spun her around like her father had just spun her.

His heart swelling with even more love for the woman who was beautiful inside and out, Hart started toward them. But before he could join them, Ben Thompson gripped his arm.

"How did you get her to come here?" he asked. "She was so convinced that it wouldn't be safe."

"It is," Hart said. "And so is she."

"But Luther Mills…" Ben's voice cracked with fear. "He's a killer."

Hart nodded. "But he has no reason to kill her now. She doesn't know where the evidence is."

"What do you mean?" he asked.

"She turned it over to the chief," Hart said.

Ben chuckled and slid his arm around Hart's shoulders. His dad had died so long ago that Hart barely remembered him. But he had a feeling he was going to find out what it was like to have a father. "How'd you manage that?" he asked. "My daughter is a stubborn one."

"She's also a loving one," he said. He nodded to where she stood with Felicity in her arms. "She did it for her."

Ben squeezed his shoulders as his eyes filled with tears. His weren't the only ones.

Hart could barely see the two women through the sudden rush of moisture in his eyes. His heart ached to join them, but he had more to tell her father. He had to be honest with him.

"She will still have to testify," he said. "So we'll need to stay here until the trial. All of us."

"That's wonderful!" Margaret said as she joined them inside the house. She threw her arms around Hart. "Thank you so much for making my daughter so happy."

Hart blinked hard. "She's the one who's made me happy." Happier than he'd ever thought he could be.

Felicity caught sight of him and squealed, "Daddy! Daddy's here!" And suddenly she was climbing all over him with her muddy hands.

He laughed and caught her close. As Wendy joined them, he wrapped an arm around her and pulled her into their embrace. For so long it had been just him and his daughter. But now he knew that no matter what happened, his little girl would never be alone.

She had family now.

They were a family now.

"Your bodyguards have a tendency for getting a little too personally involved," the chief said as he leaned back in his desk chair.

Parker nodded in agreement. But he was unrepentant. "That's why you hired my division of the agency," he reminded his stepfather. "Because this assignment— because Luther Mills—is personal for all of us."

"It's more than that," Woodrow said. "They're not just invested in making sure that Mills is finally put away for all the crimes he's committed."

Parker arched a brow. "Then what is it?"

Woodrow stared at him until Parker shifted slightly in his chair. He'd begun to feel like he was in the principal's office again, about to get blamed for something he hadn't done. Or maybe something that he had...

"You're more like your mother than I realized," Woodrow said.

Parker furrowed his brow. "What are you talking about?"

"The way you've matched up your bodyguards with the people they're supposed to be protecting."

"Are protecting," Parker reminded him.

Despite his best efforts, Luther Mills had not managed to take out or to intimidate the witness or the evidence tech.

Woodrow nodded in agreement. "True. So far…"

Parker knew it wasn't over yet. It wouldn't be over until after the trial, until after Luther Mills's long-overdue conviction.

"So what's the issue?" Parker asked. "Why are you saying I'm like my mother?" Had his stepfather found out that Parker had some experience with that damn sixth sense thing that his mom had?

Even now his gut was starting to tighten up again. Rosie Mendez and Wendy Thompson were safe, though. So it had to be about someone else.

Maybe it was about Woodrow. The chief had taken possession of the evidence, and he'd made damn certain that everyone within the department knew he had it.

Yet he didn't seem worried. Instead he was grinning. "You're like your mother because you've been playing matchmaker."

Parker shook his head. "No. No way…"

"Clint and Rosie," Woodrow said. "Hart and Wendy." He ticked off his fingers.

But he would have to stop with those two. There wouldn't be any more.

Parker laughed. "That was…" Well, he didn't know exactly what that was. "I didn't do that on purpose." Or at least he hadn't thought he had. "But it's not going to happen again."

Certainly not with Tyce Jackson and the judge's daughter, Bella Holmes. The socialite heiress had nothing in common with the ex-vice cop.

And there was no way Landon Myers would ever be interested in the assistant district attorney; he didn't even trust her.

Even Keeli Abbott was more likely to kill Detective Dubridge than Luther was.

He chuckled. "Yeah, that won't be happening again…"

* * * * *

Don't miss the next Bachelor Bodyguards book,
available April 2020
from Harlequin Romantic Suspense!

And catch up with the rest of the
Payne Protection Agency in these other
thrilling romances:

Guarding His Witness
Soldier Bodyguard
In the Bodyguard's Arms
Single Mom's Bodyguard

Available now wherever
Harlequin Romantic Suspense books
and ebooks are sold!

WE HOPE YOU ENJOYED THIS BOOK!

HARLEQUIN®

ROMANTIC suspense

Experience the rush of thrilling adventure, captivating mystery and unexpected romance.

Discover four new books every month, available wherever books are sold!

HRSHALO2019

Get 4 FREE REWARDS!

We'll send you 2 FREE Books plus 2 FREE Mystery Gifts.

Harlequin® Romantic Suspense books feature heart-racing sensuality and the promise of a sweeping romance set against the backdrop of suspense.

FREE
Value Over
$20

The memories flooded back so fast and hard, slamming
into him like a physical blow, that he stumbled behind
Anna, and had to catch himself with a hand against the
wall.

How could he have forgotten all of that stuff?

Anna stopped abruptly in what looked like a dining
room and turned to face him, tipping up her face
expectantly to the light. The curve of her cheek was
worthy of a Rembrandt painting, plump like a child's and
angular like a woman's. How was that possible?

"Well?" she demanded.

"Uh, well what?" he mumbled.

"Are my pupils all right?"

He frowned and looked into her eyes. They were
cinnamon-hued, the color of a chestnut horse in sunshine,

with streaks of gold running through them. Her lashes were dark and long, fanning across her cheeks as lightly as strands of silk.

Pupils. Compare diameters. Even or uneven. Cripes. His entire brain had just melted and drained out his ear. One look into her big innocent eyes, and he was toast. Belatedly, he held up a hand in front of her face, blocking the direct light.

She froze at the abrupt movement of his hand, and he did the same. Where was the threat? When one of his teammates went completely still like that, it meant a dire threat was far too close to all of them. Without moving his head, he let his gaze range around the room. Everything was still, and only the sounds of a vintage disco dance tune broke the silence.

He looked back at her questioningly. What had her so on edge? Only peripherally did he register that, on cue, the black disks of her pupils had grown to encompass the lighter brown of her irises. He took his hand away, and her pupils contracted quickly.

"Um, yeah. Your eyes look okay," he murmured. "Do you have a headache?"

"Yes, but it's from all the sanding I have to do and not from my tumble off your porch."

Don't miss
Navy SEAL's Deadly Secret *by Cindy Dees,*
available January 2020 wherever
Harlequin® Romantic Suspense
books and ebooks are sold.

Harlequin.com

HRSEXP1219

HARLEQUIN®

ROMANTIC suspense

Heart-racing romance, breathless suspense

**When an earth-shattering revelation upends
their billion-dollar company, the Colton family of
Mustang Valley, Arizona, must track down the person
attempting to sabotage their every move.**

**Look out for the first two books in the series!
Available January 2020**

www.Harlequin.com